CLOCKWORK SISTER

M E RODMAN

LUNA NOVELLA #6

Text Copyright © 2021 M E Rodman
Cover © 2021 Jay Johnstone

First published by Luna Press Publishing, Edinburgh, 2021

A CIP catalogue record is available from the British Library

www.lunapresspublishing.com
ISBN-13: 978-1-913387-61-7.

For Kit

To my family, both chosen and blood,

in all their wonderous weirdness.

I love you more than I can say.

Contents

Chapter One

The black lacquer-wood coffin of Mara a'Tam, eighth princess of the Tamyin Dynasty rumbled slowly along the heart-vein of the city towards the distant spires of the imperial tombs. Behind it the many leaves of the Empress's Bridge folded back against each other with well-oiled precision, separating the island of the Imperial Palace from Tam City once again.

The heart-vein was lined with citizens, each one standing with their heads bowed. Silence shrouded the path, broken only by the hollow thud of the funeral drum as it beat out its rhythm. Black streamers whirled in gusting winds from open windows, swathes of black cloth covered the doors of the houses and shops that ran along the vein. The colour of mourning scattered through the capital.

Mourning for a woman no one in the city had ever seen.

Aeon's hands clenched briefly inside the pockets of her coat. The master of ceremonies had placed her directly behind the cart, close enough to touch the coffin's slick, polished surface. She walked at the head of five hundred imperial courtiers and did not look back. The courtiers were silent too, affording the princess more respect in death than they ever had in life. Aeon supposed she should have been bitter about that, but all she felt was numb.

Nothing seemed real, not the coffin, not the drum, not the ground beneath her feet, not the crowds that watched in silence. The sky above was heavy with cloud, a promise of rain in a wind that was damp and cold and blew along the broad passage of the heart-vein with enough force to tug at the elaborate headdresses and black mourning streamers that adorned the procession.

The elaborate arches of the Bone Bridge reared up ahead, pale against the shadowed sky. The parapet was lined by bridge guards in black and red livery, iron-tipped spears in their hands. They stood straight, heads up, in proud salute to the cavalcade's approach. The Bone Bridge was the longest of the Maker's bridges, stretching out over a mile of northern ocean before it reached the islands of the dead.

A scattering of rain swept the crowd and Aeon shivered despite her thick, wool coat. The coffin in its creaking, straining cart rumbled across the bridge and into the imperial necropolis to the thud of the drum.

The great tombs of the Imperial Family with their golden spires and bright, red-tiled roofs stood alone on the crest of the hill. A city in miniature. A long, winding path crept up the steep incline in a lazy spiral that set the cart drivers swearing and the courtiers panting as the cavalcade picked up its pace, nearing its destination.

The paths and gardens that surrounded the tombs were immaculate, perfectly groomed by imperial gardeners. The clearings between tombs were scattered here and there by delicate wooden shelters, sides open to the elements, intricately carved and fragile as spun glass. Spaces for members of the Imperial Family and their guests to rest in when they visited.

The princess's tomb waited in the sunward side of the necropolis. It was smaller than that of her mother and aunt, sheltered behind the bulk of her elder sisters as befitted a princess who had never become a mother. Lamplight glowed in its windows and its great double doors stood waiting. Beyond them the vast stone slab where her tomb would rest, gleamed in the golden glow, marble inlaid with veins of gold.

Aeon blinked, there was rain on her face, damp on cheeks and eyes.

The cart rumbled in through the doors and out of sight, the doors closing behind it. Inside servants would be frantically lifting the coffin, carefully setting it on its bier and hurriedly wiping fingerprints and rain from its pristine surface.

Outside the court waited, silent in respect, the wind whistling past the leaning bodies of encircling tombs. Those closest to Aeon shivered. Though she could not help but notice the space that existed around her.

When the doors swung open again the coffin was in its place and the Empress herself was standing beside it. Eight imperial princesses and one prince flanked their mother. Representatives of Mara's immediate family clad entirely in black, their eyes heavily kohled, streaks of black on cheeks and chin.

The court went to its knees on the flags of the square before the tomb, heads bowed in respect and adoration. Aeon knelt expressionless. Conscious that the only mark of mourning she had chosen were the ribbons braided into her long, dark hair. She kept her hood up and her head bowed, shrinking back from the weight of the Empress's cool, dark gaze. Aware that when the Empress looked at her, she saw her dead daughter's face.

The Empress stepped forward, raising her hands and opening her mouth. Her voice spun out into the rising wind. Aeon did not hear the words. They were drowned by air and numbness. But she saw the courtiers around her rise, and followed, standing unwavering even though her legs had begun to tremble ever so slightly.

The formal words of dedication to the Dark Mother were over far too quickly. The Empress lifted her hand and the great doors of the princess's tomb closed for the last time. As one, and in silence, the court turned to follow the Imperial Family on the long walk back down the hill. Aeon stayed behind, watching the winding line with its shades of black as it moved off towards the bridge. A chill wind whipped in from the sea, leaving salt on Aeon's lips. She wiped them with trembling fingers.

There was a side entrance to the tomb, a narrow door painted the same grey as the building stone. Aeon slipped inside it, her feet echoing on the chill tiles of the polished floor. The tomb was empty, the lamps no longer lit, but the windows were unshuttered, and the pale gleam of fading daylight fell into tiled emptiness.

There was nothing in the room but the byre and its lacquered burden.

The princess's coffin was cold to the touch, the wood did not even feel like wood but ran like silk beneath Aeon's fingers.

"I'm sorry," she said, her voice echoing in the great vault of the room, dancing back to her on the stale air. "I'm sorry I couldn't save you."

She could almost imagine Mara's reply, the breadth of her smile, the way her eyes glowed with warmth. "No one could save me from this." She would have said. "No one."

It was the truth and it still hurt.

Aeon walked slowly back across the bridge leaving the dead behind her. She chose a longer, quieter route back to the palace than that of the courtier's cavalcade.

The court would be attending a sumptuous banquet followed by a melancholy evening of flute and zither. Aeon returned to her assigned room, in Mara's empty Domain and sat upon the rumpled bed. The fires were unlit, and the air was damp. Darkness filled the corners, untouched by lamplight. The silence was absolute.

No one would come back here. No servants, no courtiers, no members of the Imperial Family. A few hurried linen room staff who would strip the beds and swathe the furniture in protective cloths. The doors would be closed and locked. The windows shuttered and bolted. This place was as dead, now, as the woman who had lived here.

Aeon tried not to think about what was next. Though she knew it was coming. Her original was dead – her purpose was gone. She was ready for the end.

People said there was nothing so still as a motionless simulacra. Aeon felt her body relax into that stillness now, no movement, no breath; she did not even blink. The night folded in about her, close and cold. She did not bother to shiver. All the actions she had learnt over the years that allowed her to blend in with the court, with the princess, with the world around her. Alone, she needed none of them. Alone she was the bare bones of the thing she had been created to be.

A thing without function. A thing that had been left behind.

In the distance, music swelled from the great hall where Princess Mara's funeral night held the court in thrall. No one was thinking of the princess's empty rooms, no one was thinking of her discarded clothes or abandoned possessions. They were not thinking about her simulacra. Not yet.

Aeon drew in a breath. She didn't need to, but the reflex was built into her body. Like the reflex that caused her to draw her hand back from the heat of a flame.

She rose, walking over to stand before the mirror in the corner of the room. In the dim light the princess's face stared back at her, a perfect copy in every way. Mara's cool eyes, Mara's soft skin, Mara's long, dark hair tangled with mourning ribbons. Aeon pressed her fingers to her face, watched Mara's long, thin fingers press into Mara's soft, round cheeks.

Mara had not looked like this in the end. After months of coughing and weight loss, she had been hollow eyed and grey skinned. Her fingers sharp and brittle, her cheeks sunken and bloodless. The image in the mirror was Mara as she had been when they first met.

She was the Mara who left the sheltered walls of the inner palace to take her place in the imperial court and been gifted with her very own fetch – a simulacra built by the great Maker Larch himself. Aeon could still remember the flush of pleasure in the princess's face, the sudden warmth in her dark eyes.

Six years had passed since that day, six years during which Aeon had been Mara's shadow. Shield. Bait. And in the end the princess had coughed her life away like any unfortunate in a city slum.

The priesthood who served the All Mothers had declared often and loudly that simulacra could not board the ship that carried the dead over the great ocean beneath the Dark Mother's Gate and into her Domain. Aeon could only hope they were wrong, she could only trust that she would see her princess again after the end.

It was all she had left.

She turned away from the mirror. The room was so dark now that the furniture was nothing but shadow upon shadow. Aeon drew off her mourning clothes, unlaced the braid in her hair and brushed it out, letting it fall in wave over wave down her shoulders. She dressed instead in the plain but well-cut clothes that Mara had provided. The princess had never insisted that Aeon wore livery, though that was the common practice.

Dressed and with hair rebound, Aeon sat again, settling back into motionlessness. Waiting. Beyond the window, the sister rose, huge and golden in the starlit sky, a handspan below the arc of the Dark Mother's Gate across the northern horizon. Cold air filled the room, ghosting across Aeon's warm flesh.

The music had faded, the night was empty, silent, still.

Across the room the door handle turned, the door opened.

Aeon looked up. Lamplight flooded into the room from the open door, silhouetting the tall, dark haired figure who stood there. Uncertain. Watchful.

"Era?"

"You're here."

Aeon smiled faintly. "Yes."

Era blinked, stepping into the room and shutting the door. "You don't attend the banquet?"

Aeon shook her head. How could she attend the mourning for the princess while bearing her face?

Era sighed. She was an eerie echo of the Empress with none of her restless energy or iron strength. A replacement for the Empress's first fetch who had not survived a curse that almost took the Empress's life. She and Aeon were caul-sisters, built by the same Maker, they had shared a cauldron, and left the water at the same time. It was as close as simulacra came to family.

"The Empress will see you tomorrow."

Aeon had been expecting the summons, of course. She bowed her head, looking blindly down at her hands where they lay, pale and still in her lap.

Era crossed the room, moving in the smooth, boneless way that simulacra only used when they were alone together. She reached for Aeon's hands, cool skin cupping her fingers. When Aeon looked blindly up into her face, Era's expression was almost kind. "I can feel your pain."

Aeon shrugged. "It is nothing."

"It is never nothing; how can it be? Your original is dead and yet you are still standing."

Aeon looked away. "Will it happen...?"

Era shook her head fiercely. "No. She will return you to Maker Larch, you will be at home." She hesitated. "You know Solel, it will be easy."

It was true. Maker Larch's Apprentice had always been good to them.

And it was right, Aeon knew this. She was floating in the emptiness the princess had left behind, adrift like an abandoned boat lost among the islands. There was nothing left for her but to return to the waters from which she had come.

And yet it was so soon. Was she really ready for the darkness and what she might find there? Her hands were trembling.

"Do you think..." The words fell hesitatingly from her lips in a half-formed tumble. "If I asked, do you think she would give me a little more time?"

Era stared at her, a distant sadness in her eyes. "Her daughter is dead, Aeon, a daughter who looks, moves, sounds like you. I don't think she dares think of you walking around in the world when Mara is gone – can you blame her?"

Aeon flinched. Era was right, of course. The Empress would not choose to keep this image, this echo of her child, when the truth was locked away in a stone tomb.

A wave of fear washed over her, cold as the winter sea.

Her hands tightened around Era's fingers. "I'm not ready." It was a whisper, as if it were some kind of sin to speak the words out loud.

Era's expression was taut, but her eyes were warm. "You will be, Sister," she said. "You will be."

#

Aeon tried for dormancy, but even lying full length on her bed, she failed. Every time she closed her eyes, she saw the cold desolation of the tomb, the grey shadows on Mara's wasted skin. She heard the princess's last rattling breath.

Every time she opened her eyes the emptiness of the room hit her like a blow. She got up, dressed and left her room, walking up two floors to where balconies overlooked the Empress's night blooming gardens. The night was cloudless and full of stars, both sister and brother rising so high their brilliance was dimmed by the gleaming arc of the Dark Mother's Gate.

Mara had loved it here.

Aeon leaned on the balustrade and watched the dance of the stars.

A rustle of movement made her turn.

A woman stood in the arched doorway. Her skin and eyes both a deep, warm brown, her mouth generous and full. Her clothes were very fine and very sombre in their mourning black.

Aeon knew her.

Tahl a'Tam, womaniser, gambler, duellist, and ninth princess of the Tamyin Dynasty. Aeon had met Mara's sister only once before; Tahl preferred the city to the palace and rarely attended court events.

She glared now, almost as if Aeon were a person, not a relic. There was pain as well as fury in her eyes. "How dare you outlive your original."

Aeon looked away. "I never meant to."

It was true. Not once in the six years she had spent by Mara's side had she contemplated living without her. That wasn't what fetches did. They served, they protected and eventually, when they met a curse they couldn't beat, they died.

Only Aeon hadn't died; she had lived. She was standing here, while Mara's body rotted beneath the obsidian lid of her coffin and her soul sailed away to the land of the dead

Aeon moved away from the parapet, her hands hanging loose by her side. Maybe if she kept her eyes lowered, respectful, she would be allowed to leave.

Tahl stepped directly into her path. "Mara was young, she was healthy. She was a princess, for Mother's sake. How could she just die like that? How could she waste away like some commoner from the dregs?" The princess was shaking.

"She was ill," Aeon said softly. "Anyone can get ill. Not even a greenwife can cure the black lung."

Tahl's face grew hard. "Or someone wanted her gone, and

who better to orchestrate that then her own fetch?"

Aeon flinched.

For a moment it seemed like the princess was going to say something else. Then she snarled like a beast at bay, turned on her heel and left. Aeon stayed on the balcony, grief, guilt and shame turning her skin cold.

#

The Empress's Domain was decorated in shades of gold that glittered coldly in the sunlight. Its entrance was guarded by a series of delicately wrought metal gates: iron, copper, silver, bronze. Aeon followed a guard through the amber glow of late morning. The blustery wind, grey clouds and chill from the day before had passed, leaving blue sky behind. They passed numerous pairs of guards, standing alert, their hands curled tight about leaf-headed spears. The palace was quiet, sombre, as befitted a funeral day.

Aeon was ushered into a receiving room. It was patterned in shades of white and jade; large windows on one side of the room overlooked still, moonlit water. The Empress sat on a raised dais at the far end of the room, her legs folded neatly before her. She was clad in the same black she had worn in the tomb, her eyes dark with kohl.

The guard stopped, bowing low before the dais.

The Empress dismissed her with the wave of a hand, and she slipped away through white silk draperies embroidered with sinuous green leaves.

Aeon faced the Empress.

They were not alone. A member of the imperial guard stood at the back of the room, his back straight, his eyes staring straight ahead.

"My daughter was fond of you." The Empress's voice was low and behind its steel, Aeon could hear the thrum of her grief.

She bowed her head, not daring to look into those keen, dark eyes.

"You have served her well."

It was comforting, after the fury of Tahl's grief to hear those words. To the Empress, at least, she had done nothing wrong. She had served her purpose well. Though she did not deserve praise. She had only done that which she was built to do. If she had not been a simulacra she would have shifted uncomfortably; instead she settled her body into utter stillness.

"Please convey my gratitude to your Maker."

Aeon bowed stiffly. "Yes, Serenity."

The Empress was silent for a time. The room was full of shadows and tears and as silent as Mara's tomb. Then she sighed and waved her hand again. A tall, hooded figure appeared at the back of yet another servant. Beneath the hood the lines of a green leather mask curved across brown skin.

"Thank you, Aeon." The Empress said quietly.

She bowed low to the Empress, stepping back the required three paces before turning to follow the hooded figure from the room. She left the Empress unmoving on the soft cushions of her dais, her face empty of everything, almost as still as that of a simulacra.

#

Aeon was led through the sunlit palace, through the many courtyards that ran in concentric lines around the Domains of the Imperial family, to the great copper-banded doors that lead to the bridge. The hooded figure was long-legged and moved with an easy, familiar lope. Aeon said nothing. It was not permitted for a simulacra to address an Apprentice or a Maker when they went masked.

The guards at the bridge examined the pass Aeon's escort proffered, a red wax seal attached to a ribbon of white silk. The bridge captain blew on the piercing whistle that set the crank teams to the windlass. The leaves of the bridge unfolded with the rumble of heavy clockwork, inching their way across shadowed waters. The light of the sun sent gold skittering along the crest of waves.

The arc of the bridge hit the far bank with a hollow thud. Aeon's escort strode out and Aeon stopped to look back at the palace one last time. High, white walls reflected the gleam of the sun, spires glinting gold above fluted turrets. There was a disturbance by the bridge door, a scrabble of fine clothes and muffled voices. Aeon turned, hurrying to catch up with her escort as he reached the smooth stones of the heart-vein. They walked skyward.

The city was alive with noise and movement, pulsing with the whirl of hundreds of bustling bodies as the citizens of the empire went about their business.

Bells tolled out the half hour, as they turned from the heart-vein onto the spine that ran like an undulating snake across the Market District. It connected Tam City's two widest bridges at the seaward and sunward ends of the city and was one of the busiest routes in the capital. Here the streets were lined with the houses of well-to-do traders and merchants, many of whom lived above their shops. Spacious two and three storey buildings built in pale stone, with windows that opened wide to let in the rich sea breezes.

Aeon followed her escort seaward towards the great glittering arch of the Silvergate Bridge.

The Maker's District was quiet and respectable, broad streets lined with cherry trees cradled the Maker's houses. Each single-storied house was set in neat gardens, walled in yellow stone topped with brightly painted wooden panelling. Alleys ran alongside for deliveries to the workshops, forges, smeltworks and birthing houses which were positioned at the back of most properties. Not everyone who lived here was a Maker, but everyone had some connection to the craft, either as a supplier or a trader of their wares.

The air was thick with the scents of metal and oil, of warm spice and still water. It was familiar and safe, and Aeon slowed her pace, letting her escort move ahead.

She was home.

The house of Maker Larch stood on the corner of Ochre Street, a short walk from the filigree gate that gave the district bridge its name. Its double doors were painted blue and gold and hung with black mourning streamers.

"Come." Aeon's escort spoke for the first time, striding up the short flight of steps to bang on the door. After a moment the door opened a short distance and a servant in dull brown, an apron wrapped about his waist, peered out.

"Master Solel!" His voice was thin and reedy, and he bowed, blinking owlishly out into the dazzling light. His eyes were the same nondescript colour as his apron.

Aeon's escort pushed down his hood and pulled away his mask, a cheerful smile drawing an answering grimace from Aeon. Of course, it was Solel.

"Bleak." Solel replied warmly.

Aeon wasn't sure but she could have almost sworn that the doorman blushed.

The door was flung open, Bleak bowing even lower, before leading them across a courtyard and into a comfortable receiving room. Master Maker would be informed of Master Solel's arrival, he declared, and refreshments brought. Then he left them. He did not once glance in Aeon's direction.

The room was simple and yet richly decorated. Fine silks, bright metals and expensive ceramics filled the lamplit space. The colours were cool and muted. A brazier had been placed in one corner to take the edge off the lingering night's chill.

Aeon studied Maker Larch's Apprentice as he crossed the room. He was older than the last time that Aeon had seen him, but his boyish smile was the same, as were his careful hands and the way he folded his long body into a chair.

Refreshments arrived, khvā, spiced tea and plates of small, round cakes sticky with honey. Solel filled his plate and Aeon accepted a cup of khvā even though she wasn't hungry.

Moments later the door opened to admit a tall, slightly stooped man with greying hair and a pair of bright, bright blue eyes. Aeon abandoned the khvā and rose, bowing low. While Solel grinned and stepped forward to grip the man's hand.

"Master."

"Solel." The Maker's voice was deep and smooth, like the depths of the ocean, "It's good to have you back. How was Spire Ridge?"

Solel shrugged. "An easy fix, Master. I picked our Aeon up on the way back." He spread brown hands wide in a graceful gesture.

The Maker smiled softly, nodding as Aeon bowed again.

She felt her face flush. It was awkward, to see her Maker after years at court. He was older too, his face more lined, his hair white rather than grey. He had always seemed eternal, as ageless as stone.

"It is good to see you, Aeon."

"And you, Maker."

She felt his bright gaze run across her body, his expression considering.

"Was the Empress pleased with your service?"

Sunlight flooded the room. Yesterday she had watched as Mara was locked away in a cold, black tomb. Today, she was new-born again and facing her Maker.

"Yes," she said.

His smile widened. "Then I am proud too." His smile faded like the sunlight. "You understand what comes now?"

She could not speak; her mouth was dry. She nodded.

"I'm sorry, child, but the contract was very specific."

Aeon bowed her head. "I understand."

"I must speak with Solel about his trip," the Maker continued. "Finish your khvā, take a walk around the gardens, make your goodbyes. Come to the workshop at four this afternoon."

Aeon bowed as the Maker led his Apprentice away.

She did finish her cup and drained another. The Maker's private gardens were bright with flowers and sweet with heavy scents. Sunlight broke through the clouds and lit up every corner of the small, walled expanse. She did not say goodbye. Era was at the palace and Mara was gone — there was no one else.

Just before three Maker Larch left his study and she thought for a moment he was coming to see her. But he was masked and in a hurry, moving with a speed that belied his apparent age and he passed her without speaking.

Bells tolled the hour, a cacophony with every great clock in the city adding its voice as Aeon made her way to the workshop.

The room was familiar, full of the clutter of the Maker's craft, gears and chains spread across scored and scorched worktables; glass bottles filled narrow shelves across every wall. A bare metal bench lay waiting, Solel standing patiently beside it.

He glanced across at her as she entered. "I hope you had a pleasant afternoon." His smile turned wry, "Despite the circumstances."

"I did. "Aeon replied.

"Good. Please, lie down, I shall make this as painless as I can."

Aeon trusted him enough to be sure he would try. She wondered what it would be like – to end. Would it hurt? Would she see Mara again? Aeon chocked down the bitterness that rose in her mouth and threatened to drown her.

She lay down upon the bench and Solel drew a chair in close. A glass and bronze syringe gleamed where it lay on the worktable beside him. Its silver tipped needle glinting. The solution inside was the quicksilver-grey of mercury.

Solel's blue gaze held hers for a moment. "Are you ready?" he said at last.

She nodded. She did not look away.

Solel picked up the syringe. "This may sting a little," he said.

Aeon let her body fall into stillness, as Solel busied himself with her arm. The pain of the injection would come, and it would go. She would endure it.

The needle bit and she refused to react. She would not stiffen or flinch. She was a simulacra, she controlled her own body. Aeon's eyelids were already drooping when the needle slid out of her skin. Her chest felt tight and her breath was laboured. Her limbs were suddenly too heavy, she could not move them, she did not control anything after all. She should have panicked but all she felt was a weariness that swept over her, thick and black as smoke.

She closed her eyes.

#

She was on fire, her body burning, pain dragged its way into her throat and Aeon realised she was screaming. She struggled to open her eyes, but she couldn't move. Darkness was drowning her, pressing on her chest, crushing her arms and legs. She tried to call for help, to find words within the screams filling her mouth.

In the distance she thought she heard voices, mutters and swearing. Solel's soft tones sounding sharper than she had ever heard them. But she couldn't be sure, and, in the end, there was nothing but pain and fear and the crushing depths of the dark.

#

"Careful."

"Why?" A thin, bitter whine.

"Because I don't want to ruin my back."

"You could carry her one handed, I expect, Master." The

words were sly.

"Shut up."

"Didn't work then."

"No."

"At this rate, there'll be more in the pool than out of it."

"It will work." The voice hard as though through clenched teeth. "We'll keep trying."

#

Aeon half opened her eyes. The pain had gone, though it lingered in her memory. She blinked a few times before realising that she was peering up into the night sky. Cold wind blew through the darkness, sending a shiver across her skin - her naked skin.

Aeon moved an arm, carefully inching it into the world around her. Her fingers settled on something slick and cold like the body of a dead fish. She hurriedly pulled back her fingers. Beneath her she felt damp, rain-slicked wood, but when she tried to raise her head, she discovered she could barely lift it. The effort left her panting and wincing with pain as she pulled on muscles that were too weak to aid her.

She blinked again and stared up into a sky just visible over the high, brick wall. Stars gleamed briefly, paling against the golden glow of the sister, hanging heavy and round bellied and almost full. Lower and smaller, the brother was a blue-white crescent. Aeon could not see the sprawling curve of the Dark Mother's Gate from where she lay.

A spatter of rain squalled across Aeon's face and she flinched, swearing under her breath. She turned her head to the side. There was a face next to hers. Its features were slack, empty flesh that only bore the semblance of life now. Dead eyes filmed with the pale skin of burgeoning decay, stared straight into Aeon's face.

She jerked back, a choked sound of distress bubbling from her throat. There were maggots spilling out of that gaping mouth.

The involuntary movement seemed to break something inside her. She scrambled to her feet, weaving where she stood. Stumbling towards the outlines of the door at the back of the yard. Light seeped in under it, the golden glow of a streetlamp. She was in the back of her Maker's house, in the flagged courtyard where the workshops and birthing house stood. A silent yard, unlit and defiled by a handcart full of corpses.

The smell of decay filled every breath she drew into her gasping lungs as she reached the door. It was bolted from within - it was late enough that the house servants would have closed up the yard. But the bolts were well-oiled and well used. She slid them open with grasping fingers, the sky tilting above her head as she thrust at the door and tumbled out into the mud of the alley.

Her body tightened, a wash of pain rippling through it. Her fingers dug into the soaked soil, mud embedding itself in her nails. The shadows of the alley were filled with a noise and it took her a moment to realise it was her own desperate gasping. She tried to rise but fell again, her knees thudding down into the slick wetness that felt as if it was just waiting envelope her. There was no way out of this; she was trapped. What would Solel think when they found her here in the morning, gasping and flailing like a worm drawn out by the rain? She was supposed to be at an end. Would they end her all over again?

Something half remembered tugged at her, words that had been spoken above her head and suddenly she was afraid. She didn't want them to find her. She didn't want to go back into that yard.

She tried to rise again only to slip sideways and down onto her side.

In the stillness of a city in curfew she heard the sound of soft booted feet. They were coming towards her, quiet as a whisper.

She could not run.

She could not get up.

There was a figure standing over her, a dark hood hiding a pale face, a pair of cool grey eyes. And then there was nothing. The darkness had dragged her back down.

Chapter Two

"You look pretty." Mara was teasing, a hint of mischief alight in her eyes. "You should wear it for the evening."

Aeon stepped back from the mirror and everything she could see in the glass. The sleeveless nature and low neckline of the gown showed the green, red and gold lines of the inked brands that covered her arms from shoulder to wrist. The rest of it fitted perfectly, outlining the smooth lines of her body. "I couldn't possibly. It wouldn't be right."

Mara laughed again, brushing dark hair impatiently from her face. "But it would help me immensely."

Aeon turned a frown of deep disapproval on the princess. "I might share your face, Highness but that does not mean I can be you at functions you don't wish to attend."

Mara sighed, looking mildly aggrieved. "Why do you always have to be so…you," she said.

#

Pale morning light fell through a nearby window and the air was thick with the taste of brine. The ceiling above her was of rough, weathered wood and reed thatch, dark beams so close to her head it felt as if she could reach up a hand and touch them. A foot away two walls met in a rough corner.

Aeon glanced down. She was lying on a thin sleeping mat with a blanket draped over her. A lurch of confusion and panic surged under her ribs. The room was small and dirty with slanted walls and one small, grimy window. It was utterly unfamiliar.

A horn cup of clean water sat on the floor beside the sleeping mat. She emptied it without taking a breath, her mouth was dry with foulness and her throat ached.

What was this place? Not even servants slept in such ragged quarters. The wind whistled eerily round the eaves, singing through the shingles and gusting through gaps in the wooden cladding.

Aeon climbed unsteadily to her feet and walked over to the window. She looked down onto the weathered slate of a short pier built out over the water. Abandoned pilings jutted from the water on either side. The water was sluggish and oily in places, pocked with drifts of unnamed rubbish.

Where was she? Why was she here? She glanced down. Why was she naked? Why…?

She stood and stared at her arms. Where the twining imprint of brands had woven, red, green and gold, there was nothing but smooth, pale skin. She reached out with trembling fingers; she could feel the hard ridges of the escapement beneath her skin, but the intricate inked markings of a fetch were utterly gone.

Bewildered and shivering in the damp air, she hurried back to the sleeping mat, grabbing the quilt, worn threadbare but still warm and wrapping it about her shoulders.

She must have made some sound for the door opened and a slight figure clad in faded grey-brown stepped into the room. They nodded in greeting, left hand over their heart. A green curl of verdigris ink ran along their third finger, but their pinched features were largely indistinct in the dim light. All except the red stain that crossed their right cheek and rose to encircle the eye. They moved like a simulacra and held a bundle of cloth under one arm.

Aeon glared up defiantly from the floor, feeling foolish. Her stomach was cold, her heartbeat loud in her ears and she couldn't still the threat of panic rising in her throat. "What do you want with me?"

The simulacra frowned, their grey eyes hard. "What makes you think I want anything. If it wasn't for me, you'd be dead right now."

Aeon pulled the quilt closer. "I don't understand."

The simulacra sighed, tossing the bundle into Aeon's lap. "Get dressed, come down to the kitchen and I'll tell you all about it."

They walked from the room as silently as they had entered.

Aeon watched them leave. Despite a Maker's skill, some simulacra came out of the chrysalis warped or marked, ruined and uncontractable. A nix. The stain on the simulacra's face meant they could never serve an original. Not because of any lack in skill or ability, but because no one would pay the rates a Maker charged for something so flawed. Just looking at them made Aeon feel subtly uncomfortable. She had always wondered what happened to nixes, but she didn't know what to make of this. Where was their Maker? A sudden chill rushed up Aeon's spine. The nix didn't have one. They were a rogue, running from their Maker and at the mercy of hired hunters.

Aeon opened the bundle. The clothes inside were plain and serviceable, an undyed linen shirt that had been patched more than once, wool breeches and jerkin, stained stockings with drawstring ties to hold them up under the cuff of the breeches, a pair of low heeled boots and a thick, woollen coat. The coat was better quality than the rest, it was lined, warm, with deep pockets and a heavy hood. Aeon noted there was cuts in its skirt to accommodate the hilt of a blade.

Mara's hair had fallen to her knees and after six years Aeon had become used to managing it. She brushed it back into a hasty braid, tying it with a scrap of rope she found discarded in a corner of the room.

She made her way carefully down to the bottom of the house. There were three storeys and several uneven staircases, and her legs were shaking by the time she reached the ground floor. Her muscles ached and intermittent pain flared under her skin like tongues of flame. What had happened to her? Why wasn't she at an end?

The rest of the house was much like Aeon's room, wood settled beneath her feet in shivers and low creaks. The walls were crooked, unpainted and damp. The wind whistled across the angles of the roof, singing from the corners of each room as she passed.

At last she found her way into the kitchen. It held little more than a large wooden table, stained and marked with an array of scars and cracks. A long bench was set on either side. On the far end of the room, a grate, thick with peat, heated a kettle hanging from a hook over the flames.

The nix was at the table, a cup held between long-fingered hands. The sweet, cloying scent of khvā filled the room.

They looked up as Aeon stepped hesitantly into the room. "Hungry?"

Aeon nodded diffidently. "Where am I?"

The nix rose, moving leisurely towards the kettle and the small table set beside the grate. There was an enamel tin and a green-stained spoon lying there. They measured out a portion of green powder into a cup and lifted the kettle with a cloth about its iron handle.

"Swallow Street, in the dregs," they said.

"Why did you bring me here?"

The nix shrugged, setting the cup down on the opposite side of the table and retaking their seat. "You'd rather I left you there to die?"

"Die?"

Heat flared through Aeon's body again, and she sat down rather shakily. "What do you mean, die?"

"Cease to exist, become eternally dormant, wake no more. What do you think I mean?"

"To end. I understand that." Aeon frowned. "I expected… that. Why haven't I ended?"

The nix eyed her warily for a moment and then shrugged. "Because your Maker fucked up, I suppose."

Aeon stiffened. "My Maker is one of the most distinguished in the city. He has contracts with nobles, with royalty."

"No doubt," the nix said wryly. "But everyone makes mistakes. I'm sorry, what is your name?"

"Aeon, I'm called Aeon."

"Naevus."

Aeon tried to smile but she couldn't seem to remember how.

Naevus sighed. "You were ended?"

Aeon looked down at the table. "My original…died. My contract stated that I was to be ended rather than sold to anyone else."

Naevus swore very quietly under their breath.

"Why do you ask?" Aeon glanced up at the nix's face.

Naevus's eyes were painfully sincere. "Because, if I didn't know any better, I'd say you were resisting the change."

When Aeon simply stared at them blankly the nix went on. "It happens sometimes. You're purged of one original and imprinted with another, only it doesn't stick, your body rejects the change. It hurts like having a bridge dropped on you, but it gets better – usually."

"Usually?"

"Unless you die."

Aeon felt anger rise hot and hungry to overwhelm fear. "You're wrong. I was ended, I don't know why it didn't work."

"Ending is easy, all Makers master that skill early on. How else do they get rid of their mistakes?" Naevus shook their head. "They were doing something else with you."

Aeon turned her face away. She didn't believe it.

"Whatever happened, you got yourself out of that yard before you joined those corpses, so I guess you were not ready to give up just yet." Naevus's tone was sharp.

Corpses. Aeon felt again the waxy coldness of pale fingers under her own. Dead eyes clouded and viscous as they stared at her through the dark. Maggots.

Naevus grinned, there was no humour to it. "They were going to feed you to the birthing pool, to make growing liquid for the cauldrons."

Aeon pushed her cup away untouched, feeling abruptly ill. "How did you…why did you?"

Naevus looked away, they seemed almost embarrassed. "It's just something we do…us rogues. We try not to leave one of our own behind."

"I'm not your own," Aeon said. "And I'm no rogue."

Naevus narrowed their eyes. "If not ours, then whose? And you ran from your Maker, didn't you?"

#

There were four other rogue simulacra in the narrow house besides Naevus. They arrived in the kitchen for their morning khvā shortly after Naevus's revelation.

Glint, a fetch who was currently imprinted on a tall, slim boy with copper curls, hired himself out to anyone who feared a curse-working. Apparently, this was a surprisingly large amount of people in the poor and merchant districts. Glint was of the opinion that maybe one in a hundred of his employers were in danger of actually being cursed but he took their money anyway. The boy was his latest original, the son of a rich merchant who was in a heated bidding war with a rival and was afraid of repercussions on his family. According to Glint, he had his own legitimate simulacra but was too cheap to pay full price to protect his loved ones.

Glint's caul-sister, Talon, had been hired to provide similar protection to the merchant's daughter. The pair of them went out early, after a hurried breakfast.

Roe and Sixfingers came down long after the first flush of dawn had faded. They shared a room on the second floor. Roe was an imago and worked at a doxy house over in the Scarlet District, where he provided a unique service. Apparently, it was possible to overlay a base imprint with a secondary one for a few hours. A scrap of skin, a shaft of hair or a mouthful of blood, and Roe could be anyone a Patron desired. According to Sixfingers, he was very popular.

Sixfingers was a nix like Naevus, with six fingers on her right hand. She was tall and broad shouldered, with a hard, pitted face, sharp, hazel eyes and, when she greeted Aeon politely, left hand over heart, revealed a spiral of verdigris prominently displayed on her first finger. The body had belonged to a very masculine bridge captain she'd imprinted on years ago and never purged her way out of. She claimed she was used to it now.

"How long have you worn it?" Aeon wondered what it would be like to keep Mara's face, to be that self for an eternity.

Sixfingers shrugged. "Must be fourteen years. The poor fool had run up bad gambling debts and really did have a curse-worker after him."

"What happened?" Aeon asked, helpfully refilling Sixfingers' cup. Roe wasn't hungry.

"The curse came down of course. It hurt like buggery." Sixfingers grunted. "But he paid and that's all I cared for at the time."

"He didn't mind about..." Aeon nodded towards Sixfingers' hand.

She grimaced. "Soldiers can't afford to be picky. A perfect simulacra would have cost him more than a year's pay. Anyway, that was the last imprint I agreed to so," Six-finger's shrugged, "This is what I'm left with, unless I want to play Roe's game."

Roe turned his head to smile up at her. "I'm not complaining," he said.

Sixfingers smirked.

Roe rose shortly afterwards, murmured something about clothes and wandered off. Sixfingers watched him go under heavy lids.

"Are you and he...?"

Aeon wasn't sure how she felt about that. Fetches were not generally expected or allowed to become close to anyone, either originals or other simulacra. It was distracting and usually considered a breach of contract. Maybe that didn't apply to imagoes who were neither branded nor implanted with a fetch's escapement, who were not expected to serve and die.

Sixfingers considered Aeon steadily. "What of it?" she said, and Aeon drew back at her tone, finding herself with nothing else to say.

She turned to Naevus, who had been quiet while the others were introducing themselves.

The bright light streaming through the kitchen windows gave a strange unfinished quality to Naevus's features. Their mouth didn't move quite right, their expressions either too fast or too slow. Their fingers were overlong, each one bearing an extra joint and the hair that fell to their shoulders was the grey of sea-soiled bone.

They glanced up and saw Aeon staring. Aeon felt her face flush at the nix's knowing glance. "Yes, I'm not imprinted. I never have been." Their expression twisted again, into something less readable. "It doesn't...stick. I look just the way I did when I clawed my way out of my chrysalis."

Aeon knew then why Naevus's features were both familiar and strange. She had looked like that once – so long ago she could barely remember it.

"What do you do, if you can't…change?"

Naevus shrugged. "Any number of things. There is plenty in a simulacra's nature that is useful even if they can't imprint."

"I hire myself out to thugs who want a little more weight." Sixfingers explained. "And Naevus thieves for them."

Aeon stared at the nix. "What?"

Naevus sighed. "Sixfingers is a fist. Plenty of petty criminals and would-be clan lords who'll pay for someone who heals quick, dies slow and knows how to scare the shit out of people." They grinned. "And I break into houses in the middle of curfew. Why do you think I was sneaking around the Maker's district?"

Aeon hadn't really thought.

She glanced across at Sixfingers. The fist was staring down at the empty cup in her hands. "Were you there, last night?"

Sixfingers grimaced. "Naevus found me and Glint at the Moth." Sixfingers cast a warm glance towards the other nix. "They were worn out from dragging you in and out of boats. Took us an hour to get you round the corner, you kept seizing."

"I what?"

"Like I told you, your body was fighting the change." Naevus said coolly.

Fire running across her skin. Pain and darkness.

"We had a friend look at you when we got back. He said you had been close to death, maybe even died a little and come back, sometime before I found you."

Aeon found herself nodding, she wasn't sure why. Her hands were gripping the tabletop so tight it hurt.

Naevus laid a hand on her arm. "Calm down," they said softly.

Aeon drew in a deep breath, but it was as if Naevus's touch had sparked something. The heat was growing, becoming flames. The burning was travelling up her legs, devouring her skin, charring her bones. Her breath, when she dragged in another one, was searing.

In the distance she heard swearing and a panicked shout. Pale hands were gripping her shoulders.

"Aeon, hold on." Naevus's voice fought to cut through the flames.

Aeon squeezed her eyes shut.

"Hold on, now." It was a new voice, not one she remembered hearing before. There was a sudden stab of pain in one arm, sharp as the point of a needle.

"Just breathe." The new voice said, and Aeon looked up into a pair of brilliant, flaring green eyes.

She felt a newfound terror flare deep inside her and if she had had any strength at all, she would have pulled away then, she would have staggered to her feet and fled. But she couldn't, she was trapped, helpless, soaked in pain and bound beneath the cursed gaze of her enemy.

#

Aeon opened her eyes. She was lying on a couch in an unfamiliar room, though by the damp-slicked, crooked walls she knew it was still the house on Swallow Street. She bolted upright and found herself face to face with a mass of dark curls, a narrow, sharp featured face and the blazing, viridian-bright gaze of a greenwife.

Aeon swallowed and pulled back, hitting the couch behind her hard enough to jolt her aching head. "What do you want?"

The greenwife didn't move, though he watched Aeon steadily. "How are you feeling?"

Aeon fought not to wince. "I'm fine."

The greenwife nodded. "You'll feel sore for a little while, but it should pass."

Aeon frowned. "What did you do?"

"Gave you something to counteract your body's attempts to change. It's not a perfect cure but it should give you time for the imprinting shot to leave your body."

"You've seen this before?"

The greenwife frowned, viridescent eyes glowing in the dim light. "Yes, though not often."

Aeon snorted.

"You should be fine in a day or two."

"Thanks."

The greenwife smiled faintly. "It's what I do." He rose then but hesitated before leaving, as if he saw something in Aeon's face. "Was there anything else?"

"The brands on my arms." Aeon found she was stuttering as she rolled back the sleeves of her shirt.

The greenwife frowned down at the pale, unmarked skin.

"I'm a fetch." Aeon said, indignantly. "And they're just gone."

"I don't know." The greenwife said slowly, almost reluctantly. "A side-effect of your enforced change would be my best guess."

He slipped from the room then, leaving Aeon feeling both frustrated and relieved. Sixfingers poked her head round the door a moment later. The concern on her face was warming.

"I thought you were gone for sure; you were flopping about like a landed fish."

Aeon shook her head. "Not yet."

"Good."

Aeon hesitated. "Where did the greenwife come from?"

"Sena?" Sixfingers grunted. "He lives here."

Left alone on the couch to recuperate, Aeon contemplated the reality of living in the same house as a curse-worker. A greenwife.

Her stomach jolted, the reaction visceral.

Fetches were created to protect their originals against the attacks of greenwives, the terrible, murderous magics of curse-working that could kill and maim as easily as they could heal and renew. Aeon herself had diverted two attacks on Mara. She remembered little about them save the terrible, burning of her brands as they lit up across her body and a slicing pain as the wheels and gears of the escapement buried beneath her flesh rose to the surface. Mara's voice in the distance, franticly calling her name. One such attack had killed the Empress's former fetch; the one Era had replaced.

Many born with viridian eyes were strangled at birth. After all, who would keep such a treacherous child? It was well known that greenwives were unscrupulous, they would curse anyone if the reward was high enough. Just as it was true that they were profoundly able healers, blessed by the touch of their goddess.

This one just saved your life.

She wasn't sure she could understand the nature of a world where a greenwife lived in a house full of simulacra. It seemed too impossible to be true.

Even if they're not all fetches, how can they stand it?

But then nothing about this place was as you might expect. No Maker, no contracts, no originals to protect, except by choice. Aeon had not seen a single coin from the Imperial contract that had given her to Mara. Such deals were between Maker and patron, not between patron and simulacra.

They left me in a pile of corpses. Solel left me. Maker left me.

A surge of heat flared under Aeon's skin and she forced herself to relax, drawing in slow, steadying breaths.

What do I do now?

Glint, Talon and Roe still took imprints, but Aeon didn't think she could, not if this was her body's reaction. Could she become a fist like Sixfingers or a thief like Naevus? They would probably both laugh at the suggestion. Mara had been a princess, she had excelled at dancing, politics and bitterly sharp wit, not things that would help Aeon now.

Panic threatened to rise, and Aeon pushed it resolutely away. She would think of something; there had to be something.

You can always starve on the streets.

Naevus and the others might have saved her, but they had no reason to keep her, whatever Naevus said. They were strangers, not even created by the same Maker. And besides, Aeon doubted they could afford another mouth to feed.

She sat in growing darkness until Glint and Talon blew back into the house, shaking a fall of rain from their coats and demanding khvā. Aeon joined them in the kitchen, sitting back in the lamplight and listening to them laugh and gossip with Naevus and Sixfingers who sauntered in shortly afterwards.

Only Roe was missing but then Aeon supposed he worked late.

Indeed, the sister had climbed half up the sky, the brother only a step or two behind, when Roe walked into the kitchen. He was followed by a slight, brown haired simulacra with a pair of bright green eyes and a ready smile.

Naevus pushed back their chair, jumping to their feet. "Fallow, where have you been?"

The simulacra grinned mischievously, reaching a hand into a pocket in his coat. "Oh, you know." His smile turned wry. "Making money. Who's for a night at the Moth?"

There was a general chorus of assent before those bright eyes landed on Aeon.

"And who's this?"

Fallow was Roe's caul-brother, a bundle of light and life, bright and bustling in a manner that Aeon found more than a little dazzling. She wasn't the only one. It was soon clear that Fallow was the darling of the house. He even managed to root the greenwife out of his room, which Naevus informed Aeon, was a Mother's-hard thing to do.

The Moth, as it turned out, was The Black Moth, a tavern of sorts, a few streets down from the simulacra house. Gwen, the proprietor was an original, but her lover and business partner was not. Marl was an old friend of Sixfingers, having worked as a fist before Gwen took her in.

In the taproom, Fallow flashed his coin around and they settled in to drink, smoke and talk long into the night. The curfew held no sway here, where the bridges were built of wood and rope and fixed to their moorings. There were no windlass crews, no clockwork cranks, no bridge guards. This was the dregs, a scattering of islands on the skyward end of the Tam City and no one cared what happened here.

Aeon spent most of the night listening, sitting back in the shadows, but by the time they were all wending their way homewards, arms draped about each other's shoulders, she was walking with them.

Chapter Three

"It would be good if we could get hold of some wood that wasn't half rotten." Aeon said.

Naevus, leaning back against the wall of the house and squinting in a shaft of sunlight, looked dubious. "You have what you can find."

Aeon sighed.

Over the last month she had taken it upon herself to plug the holes and patch the roof of the house on Swallow Street. She had few tools to work with and even fewer materials, but it felt good to be doing something. The rest of the simulacra in the house gave her a bed every night and kept her in khvā, the least she could do was make sure the house was warm and dry.

Spring was fading into summer, bringing scattered sunlight, warmer weather, and the emergence of bugs. The smell of the water that surged around the pilings beneath the house got stronger as the temperature rose.

Aeon still didn't know what she was going to do to survive in the dregs. Thinking about it filled her with a cold sense of dread. Sometimes she woke from dreams of her other life, the sound of Mara's laughter in her ears and could not find her way back to dormancy for the rest of the night.

She was terrified of the day when Naevus turned round and demanded rent money she did not have.

Naevus shifted, draining their mug. "Come on, let's go in, it's starting to rain."

#

Later, after the light had gone down and the sister climbed up into the sky, they gathered in the kitchen to drink khvā and complain about their day. Only Roe and Fallow were missing but then they were often late back. Roe never rushed a patron and Fallow liked to sit and drink and gossip. He had invited Aeon to come and see where he worked but Aeon disliked leaving the house. Even visiting the Moth two streets away made her nervous. She couldn't seem to forget Naevus's comment about being rogue. The nix was right, she had run from her Maker. And she knew the penalty for that – a hunter's blade in the back of her skull. A true end.

Naevus was heating a second pot of khvā when Roe burst into the kitchen. He was half carrying, half dragging Fallow, whose skin was frighteningly pale, beneath the tumbling fall of warm brown hair.

"Where's Sena?" Roe demanded, panting and wide-eyed.

"I'll get him." Glint ran from the room, his shout echoing through the house. Sixfingers hurried forward to help Roe lay his burden on the kitchen floor.

"Is he alive?" Naevus murmured from beside the fire.

Roe did not look up. "I told him not to take on two patrons

in one night."

"A split shot?" Sixfingers muttered, loosening Fallow's jerkin. "I hate how you use that stuff."

"Hey," Roe protested. "I'm not the one on the floor."

Sixfingers's face remained dark. "You could be."

"What happened?" Sena was at the door, an anxious looking Glint a pace behind.

"A bad split shot," Roe said without preamble.

Sena swore very quietly, under his breath. "Alright, move out of the way."

Aeon stepped back straight away, followed by Sixfingers and a reluctant Roe. "His borrowed face dropped away half an hour ago." Roe's voice was shaking. "I thought that would be the end of it, then he just collapsed. I can't wake him."

Sena smiled tightly. "Has he done a split shot before?"

"Yes."

The greenwife stared grimly down at the still, pale figure. "Now might be a good time to start praying."

Sena worked on Fallow for most of the night, moving from tisanes poured into a half open mouth to fluid injected directly into the body and at last, as the dying hours of the night dragged the sister's golden disk from the sky, prayers that sent green wildfire spilling around his fingertips. At last he sat back on his heels, face pale and head bowed with weariness and shook his head.

Roe burst into tears.

Fallow was lifted, carried from the kitchen, and laid on a couch in the cleanest room in the house. Naevus gently covered his stillness with a blanket.

Without a word exchanged they returned to the kitchen.

Naevus filled the kettle, setting it over the grate and building up the fire underneath so that bright flames danced in the dim light.

Sixfingers had one arm wrapped about Roe's shoulder, her face grey. Roe laid his head on her shoulder and curled an arm around her waist, holding tight. Sena sat beside Naevus, Glint and Talon beside Aeon.

For a long time, they sat in silence, listening to the sounds of water rising to the boil and the hiss of flame.

"What happened?" Naevus said at last. They were looking at Sena.

The greenwife frowned. "At a guess, I would say the shot was contaminated."

He turned to Roe. "Did Fallow always get his shots from the same source?"

"Yes," Roe said instantly. "He isn't a fool." A look crossed his face and he continued more slowly. "He always used the same source… only this time there was problem. He had to go elsewhere."

"Where?" Sixfingers growled.

"I don't know; he didn't say."

Sena sighed. "Disreputable suppliers use any number of poisonous substances to eke out their product." The greenwife's gaze swept across the table. "I'm sorry, there was nothing I could do."

To Aeon's surprise he sounded genuinely remorseful.

"Roe," Naevus said quietly. "Would anyone else know where Fallow got the shot?"

Roe shifted against Six-fingers' side. "I can ask," he said.

#

Aeon had not expected to go to two funerals in little more than a month. They could not have been more different. Barely a dozen people turned out to walk behind the rumbling cart that carried Fallow's shrouded body through the narrow streets and over the creaking bridges of the lower city. The day was bright, blue skies above and a warm wind with salt in its heart.

The group, huddled together, heads down, walked in silence. Not for Fallow the grand tombs of the necropolis or the Bone Bridge. The poor of the city were burned in one of three great ovens built on the banks of the shipping district. The brick buildings were black with soot and crumbling in places. Dry plants clawed their way up through the flagstones of the outer yard.

As Fallow's brother, Roe collected the urn. He was still crying, and he wouldn't let go of Sixfingers' hand. Glint and Talon had gone to ask questions at the doxy house when everyone realised that Roe wasn't going to manage it. But the best any of the boys and girls could come up with was that Fallow had come in from Green Street that night, because he'd complained about the walk.

"Green Street? That's up in the Maker's District." Aeon couldn't keep the surprise from her tone.

Sixfingers scowled. "Of course it is."

"Our Maker lives in Green Street," Roe said quietly.

No one could find anything to say after that.

\#

After the burning, they carried Roe and the ashes back to Swallow Street.

The city streets ran in spokes and circles like the gears of a clock. Each interconnected with the other. Each ultimately ending in a bridge. There were two hundred and twenty-one bridges in all, at least officially. Some moved in cranked segments, others swung between two possible destinations as needed, others unwound flat as snakes, so low that water washed over them if tides were high. These were all evidence of the Makers' skills, each more beautiful in form and function than the last. But there were other bridges too, crafted of rough, pitted metal, or scraps of rotting wood, even lengths of knotted cord and these were built by the poor and the desperate on the dirtiest and most desolate islands of the city. They were illegal and every few years the bridge guard swept through burning or sinking them. But it was like trying to stem the ocean. The citizens needed them, and they reappeared a few short weeks after they were destroyed. Some were even built upon the burnt remains of the bridges that had gone before.

It was to these bridges that they headed, to the lost and abandoned islands where no one cared what face you wore. Where no bridge captains demanded your business or checked your pass. Where, at the end of one such bridge, built of wood and rope and painted in a thousand myriad colours, stood the narrow three-storey house Aeon was beginning to think of as home.

It stood out by itself at the end of a short pier whose supports looked none-too-safe, wooden sides weathered grey by wind and water. It was soaked in salt, its roof splattered white with gull droppings. There were no lights in any of its unshuttered windows, none of which had either glass or the scraped and oiled sheepskin that poorer folk used to attempt to block out the wilder winds and bitterest storms.

"Khvā everyone?" Naevus said with a weary smile.

They gathered in the kitchen, the simple, unglazed urn on the table between them. "Fallow and I were the first, apart from Naevus." Roe smiled faintly. His eyes were red, but he seemed calmer now the long day was done.

"I remember," Naevus said. "Didn't he fall through the roof during that storm? Landed on top of you and Sixfingers in bed, back when you had Aeon's room."

"I never did find out what he was doing up there," Sixfingers said quietly.

"He was watching the lightning," Roe said. "He loved storms."

"And snow and flowers and making people laugh," Glint said softly.

"Stealing other people's khvā, dancing in the rain, peacocks," Talon said.

Silence stole over them, but it was a restful silence, shaped by memories of their friend.

I barely knew him.

Now she never would. Aeon watched the light in the room dim and thought about the burn of a shot as it raced through flesh and bone.

I hope he felt nothing, in the end.

No one chose to be dormant that night, they sat up watching the sky grow light and the lamps splutter and die, in silence, remembering.

#

"I can go," Sixfingers said.

"No, you can't," Naevus said patiently. "We need someone who can ask questions first and use their fists second. At the very least you can't go alone."

"Well, you can't go," Sixfingers grumbled.

"Yes, thank you, I am aware of that." Naevus's tone had grown icy.

"Why can't Naevus go?" Aeon said.

They were sitting in the kitchen again. Only the three of them were awake and Naevus had said to let the others sleep. "It's been a hard few days."

Sixfingers hesitated, clearing her throat. "Naevus didn't exactly ask their Maker's permission before they left."

"Because if I had he would have slit my throat and thrown me in the pool just that much quicker."

Sixfingers glanced at Naevus from under heavy lids. "As it is, you were lucky you didn't bring a team of hunters down on you when you ran."

Aeon glanced from one to the other of them. "Would they really send hunters here?"

It was a recurring nightmare that woke her from dormancy several times a week.

Naevus's face was solemn. "Rogue simulacra give the Makers a bad name. They'd rather we were gone."

"And we undercut them," Sixfingers grunted.

Naevus grimaced, taking a long gulp from the khvā in their cup.

"I could go," Aeon said diffidently.

Sixfingers frowned. "Are you sure?"

Aeon glanced away from Sixfingers' hard gaze. "Or at least, I could go with you," she said.

#

Green Street lay at the edge of the Maker's district, beyond the carefully geared leaves of the Silvergate bridge. The bridge captain and guards wore distinctive white-gold livery and the gate from which the bridge took its name, a delicate filigree creation, awaited them at the far side of the bridge's arch, marking the entrance to the district where most of the city's craftsmen and artisans both worked and lived.

Aeon passed the turning for Ochre Street without a glance, though the skin at the back of her neck prickled at the thought of that tall brick wall and the memory of damp wood against frozen skin. Sixfingers shot a look across at her face as they moved on but said nothing.

They had chosen to go out half an hour before the curfew bell, knowing that both Maker and Apprentice would have retired to the main building, leaving the work areas to servants and lesser assistants. Roe had told them that Fallow purchased his shots at this time, which was a risk, with the curfew so close, but a calculated one. Most people in the district would be hurrying home through the shadowed streets, one more hurrying form among many would easily pass unnoticed.

Sixfingers banged on the side door, stepping back to stand against the curve of the perimeter wall. Aeon stood alone before the door, hood up, trying her best to seem scared and desperate.

The door was opened by a young, dark-skinned original,

a boy no more than sixteen, who peered apprehensively out into the night, holding onto the door with clutching fingers.

"Who's there?"

Aeon drew the hood down, tilting her face back into the cold light of the brother, riding pale and low in the sky above. Any moment now the curfew bells would start to toll.

"Oh," the boy said; even frightened it seemed he could recognise a Maker's work. "I'm afraid Devin is not working tonight."

Aeon stepped gently forward. "But you're opening the door all the same."

The boy looked away. "He didn't think anyone would come, but if they did, he asked me to…"

"That's good of you." Aeon kept her voice low and trembling. "Fallow sent me."

"Fallow?"

"I work with him in the Scarlet District. I…look, I really need…"

The boy flinched, glancing nervously up and down the street. "I don't…have anything. But Devin lives on Clattersmoke Street over in the Fabrication District. He said I could send anyone round…"

"Where on Clattersmoke?"

Clattersmoke Street backed on to Greyscale Bridge, the least beautiful of the Makers' bridges. The Fabrication District was the home to labourers, servants, factory workers and most of the industries that employed them. It never slept and at night the sky above the district shone red as ember fire. The houses that lined its streets were narrow and dirty, with cracked windows and blackened bricks. The water channels that ran under and between the wooden pilings and stony soil of the District were dark, brightened here and there by oily rainbow shimmers.

Aeon counted the houses as they passed along the street. The nervous boy had directed them to the fifth house from the corner, a tenement with doors painted red and blue. The paintwork was streaked with soot, but the colours were just visible. Devin lived on the ground floor. They approached the building; it was dark, the windows unlit by lamplight.

"Do you think he's sleeping?" Sixfingers murmured.

Aeon frowned. The curfew bell rang at the tenth hour of the night, but that seemed a little early for a young man to be asleep, even if he needed to be up early to hurry across the city to his work in another District.

"Maybe he's out."

"Dodging curfew?"

Aeon shrugged, "Plenty of people spend all night in the Scarlet District or out in the Dregs, where no one cares about the curfew."

Sixfingers sighed in agreement. "We should probably check all the same."

She walked up to the door, knocking in a subdued manner. Silence.

The door creaked gently open, falling back on rough hinges to bang against the wall. Sixfingers glanced across at Aeon, drew a blade from her boot and slipped into the darkness that waited inside. She moved surprisingly quietly for such a large person. Aeon was surprised she hadn't battered her way in shouting and slamming into things. The fist had more discretion then Naevus gave her credit for.

Aeon followed, trying to move as quietly. The house was both dark and cold, with no fire in the grate or lamps anywhere inside. The windows were unshuttered, and, through the brittle panes of oiled paper, the golden light of the sister filled the room with shadows.

Devin lay sprawled out across bare, wooden boards; at least Aeon assumed it was Devin. He was pale and motionless under the sister's light, a spill of darkness spreading out from still flesh to wash over the bare boards of the floor. Aeon reached down with tentative fingers and felt dampness beneath their tips. She swallowed a sudden surge of sickness. It was blood, cool but not yet dry. Even though she wiped her hand quickly on her breeches the feel of it clung.

Sixfingers was crouched beside the body, peering through the darkness.

"Stabbed, more than once, throat cut to make sure." Sixfingers voice was low, cautious.

Aeon glanced around the narrow, damp room. There was little in way of furnishings. A crude table and bench sat before the room's small grate, barely large enough for a griddle or cook pot. A hammock hung across the far corner; a thin blanket bundled inside it. The man's shoes stood neatly by the door and the room was clean. A kettle, hanging over the fire, was just beginning to boil. On the table, a loaf of rye bread, a lump of cheese still in its greased wrapping and a smoked eel in brown paper, sat on a clay plate, beside a horn cup. He had been about to sit down for a meal after a long day at work when someone walked in and slit his throat.

Sixfingers rose, looming in the dim light. "Whoever it was, he let them in." she said. "The door wasn't forced, and that window is far too small to climb through."

Aeon nodded. She glanced around the room again. Was this all there was? A dead man, an empty room? Fallow had been poisoned and Devin was the only one who'd known anything. Aeon felt a sudden desire to hit something.

She walked over to the fire, lifting the kettle off its hook using the rag left on the side for just such a purpose. She poured the water out to stifle the fire, before setting the kettle on the table beside the abandoned meal.

Something clinked beneath her feet.

She glanced down.

A small vial lay in the shadows under the table. Slim glass stoppered with cork. She reached down, pulling it out with trembling fingers. The liquid inside was the bright red of fresh blood.

Sixfingers drew in a breath. "A split shot."

Aeon slipped the vial into the pocket of her coat. It lay cool against jerkin and shirt. Sixfingers fumbled around beside the fireplace and pulled out a small sack which she filled with the food from the table. She grimaced when she saw Aeon's expression. "It's not needed here," she said. Then, after a considering pause, "You've never gone hungry, have you? I have friends who need this."

They left as quietly as they had arrived, leaving the door open so that Devin's remains would be found in the morning. Aeon felt bad, crouching down to close his eyes as she passed, pressing a pair of copper glints over the lids. She heard Sixfingers stop in the doorway and looked up.

"At least he'll be able to pay ship's passage to the Dark Mother's Domain."

Sixfingers shrugged but said nothing.

The long walk back to Swallow Street was accomplished in silence. Aeon wasn't sure when she had ever felt so tired, her body weary somewhere deep in her bones. Sixfingers carried the food, a permanent frown creasing her heavy brows.

"Do you think someone knows we were looking for him?" she said at last, her voice loud in the silence of curfew. They had taken a zig-zag route through the districts to avoid the bridge guards, paying a grim-faced ferryman to take them out past the bright lights of the Scarlet District to the moorings that ran along the edge of the dregs. Aeon was profoundly glad to see the rope and spit bridges of home.

She shook her head at the fist. "I think they killed him because he knew too much, and he was no longer useful." She felt the raised ridge in the line of her coat where the vial nestled. "We have to find what's in this stuff."

Sixfingers grunted. "We'll ask the greenwife."

#

Sena was sitting in the kitchen when they arrived, barely beating the dawn. Aeon watched the sister dip towards the distant horizon where gathering clouds promised rain. He looked up as they entered but he did not seem surprised. He looked tired and Aeon supposed that the last few days had taken their toll on him too. He had not attended Fallow's funeral; Naevus told them he was too tired. Aeon had not believed it, thinking him callous. But seeing the dark hollows beneath his eyes and the sharp lines on his face now, she felt ashamed.

"Did you find the man who sold Fallow that filth?" he

almost spat.

Sixfingers shook her head grimly. "Dead."

Green eyes opened wide, startled. "Dead?"

"Someone cut his throat." Aeon had never heard Sixfingers sound so dour.

She slipped a hand into her pocket and pulled out the vial. "We found this."

In the light of lamp and fire it glinted. It was neither a purging draft nor imprinting solution. Sena's heavy gaze turned to her, she felt its weight against her skin. "We think this is what he sold Fallow. We thought you might be able to find out more."

The greenwife held out a hand. She pressed the vial into his palm.

He glanced between them. "I can't make any promises," he said, "but I'll try."

#

Aeon went to her room and sought dormancy; she was bone weary, but darkness was a long time in coming. Daylight filtered through the shutters, pressing golden shadows across her bed and turning the darkness into bronze. Each time she closed her eyes, she saw coffins in carts, black streamers and the slow, grey walk of mourners. She saw tombs and chimneys and dead eyes that would not stay closed. She was so cold she could not stop shivering; it was as if since Mara's death, dying had infected her and she could not escape. Was she cursed? Was this what happened when a simulacra outlived their original? Was that why most contracts called for their end?

But you didn't go, did you? You didn't join her. You never ended.

Mara had paid her passage in gold; she had sailed under the gate long ago.

Aeon woke to a cold, grey sky and the rattle of rain against her window. She pulled on her cloths and wandered downstairs. The kitchen was warm, Naevus was sitting at the table, cup in hand.

"Are you never dormant? Is that why I always find you here?" Aeon sounded angrier than she felt.

Naevus raised a pale eyebrow. "As it happens, no, I'm not dormant for more than three or four hours a night."

"Oh," Aeon dropped her eyes, "That must be…"

"Productive?"

Aeon frowned. "Yes, I suppose so."

Naevus grinned. "You have no idea. Khvā?"

Aeon nodded. "Yes, please."

Naevus handed her a cup and sat back down. "Sixfingers told me what you found."

"Hopefully Sena can make something of it." Aeon never thought she'd have said that about a greenwife. "How did he end up living here anyway?"

Naevus tilted their head, inquiringly. "What do you mean?"

"Well, he's a greenwife. A curse-worker. Everything we were created to guard against."

Naevus snorted. "Everything you were created to guard against; not all simulacra are fetches. Besides, how do you think simulacra are made? You don't think the greenwives have a hand in it? We're life, maybe a strange kind of life, but life, and all greenwives have a hand in that."

"Really?" Aeon couldn't quite credit what she was hearing.

"You really think greenwives help Maker's to create simulacra?"

"I do." Naevus said solemnly. "Though I can see why Makers keep that particular piece of knowledge quiet. Most of their patrons are afraid of curse-workers, that's why they commission simulacra in the first place."

"Did your Maker really try to kill you?"

Naevus nodded. "I was a mistake that he didn't want to admit he'd made. He was under pressure, his patron was expecting a product and if my Maker told him what happened, if he asked for more vital ingredients, well, you know how patrons dislike parting with such things."

"They fear they will fall into the hands of curse-workers."

"Exactly. His plan was to break me down into my components, retrieve the vital parts and remake me. I'm sure I'm not the first, I was just faster than him."

Aeon shifted in her seat. "Aren't you afraid that there might be hunters after you?"

Naevus shrugged, staring down at the table. "Each day I live is one more mark in my favour and one less in his."

"Couldn't you use split shots to hide your face?"

Naevus frowned at Aeon across the rim of their cup. "No reason to think they would work any better than the imprinting. Why don't you?"

Aeon shrugged. "No one else I want to be."

Mara's face was still the last thing she saw in the mirror before she fell into dormancy, the first thing she saw in the mirror when she woke. It was something, even if the look in the eyes was never Mara's look, even if the pain on that face was never Mara's pain.

Naevus sighed. "I said I'd bring Roe up some khvā." They

rose, pushed wearily against the table and walked over to the kettle.

"How is he?"

"How would you expect? Fallow was his caul-brother, they've known each other since before they left the cauldron. They even ran together."

"Why did they run?"

"The original who commissioned Roe reneged on his payments; Roe's Maker was going to use him as an imago. Roe was terrified. I'm pretty sure Fallow just ran to keep him company."

"But Roe's an imago now."

Naevus grinned, showing those shark-like teeth. "But on his terms, fetch, on his terms. Which, you know, makes all the difference."

Sixfingers, Glint and Talon came down not long after Naevus left with Roe's khvā. Sixfingers looked as tired as Aeon felt. Glint and Talon were both pale and subdued and Aeon couldn't help noticing how they stuck close to each other, as if they were afraid to lose each other's touch for more than a moment. Their patron had nearly finished his trading deal which meant they were coming to the end of their contract. They were both looking to hunt down fresh patrons.

Aeon wonder aloud what they did about their faces in between patrons.

"Keep them, until more work comes along, it's even in our contract," Glint said. He seemed to do most of the talking.

Beside him Talon shivered. "I hate the purge shot, it burns. And I hate throwing up."

Aeon didn't know. She had been created for one patron

and one original alone. She had never been meant to wear another face.

"Fingers," Glint said, glancing across the table. "If you could put the word around that we're looking."

Sixfingers grunted in rough assent.

"We don't use split shots, so it can take a while to find new patrons," Talon explained.

"You don't? Why not?"

Talon glanced across at Glint, whose expression didn't change. "Glint had a bad reaction to a split shot we bought once. Would have died if Sena hadn't turned up in time."

Beside Aeon, Sixfingers winced.

"Did you get that shot from Green Street too?" Aeon asked.

"No," Talon said, diffidently. "From Ochre Street. From Apprentice Solel a'Vari."

#

"We need to hunt him down and demand answers."

Sixfingers looked up startled and Aeon realised she had spoken more vehemently than she'd intended. They had given the greenwife the vial two days ago and they had heard nothing. Aeon was tired of the restless pacing she couldn't quell. She'd even gone to Sena's room the night before but, according to Naevus, the greenwife hadn't made it home.

"Sometimes he stays out." Naevus said with a shrug. "He tends to fall into his work."

Greenwives were exempt from curfew, provided they marked their profession with a green sash about the waist when they answered calls for help in the early hours.

Now, in the wan morning light, Sixfingers said, "Sena rented a receiving room at the back of an apothecary's in the Market District about a month ago."

Aeon got up from the kitchen table. "Thanks."

#

Hood pulled up against the fall of chill spring rain, Aeon slipped out of the house and hurried down Swallow Street, moving along the main thoroughfare and out over the bridges that would take her to the market.

The Market District was the largest landmass in the entire city. It was split across three islands, a tumult of shops and stalls set around a series of open, flag-stoned squares known as well courts. Each court featured at least one wellhead, covered with a heavy stone seal marked with the crossed-tail seal of the water commission. All the wells in the city were owned by the state and filled by filtered rainwater. As well as keeping the wells in good working order the commission checked the purity of the water twice a day.

The centre of the market was marked by the crossing of the heart-vein and the spine. At this point the largest well in the city stood, covered in a vast stone seal. It was rumoured to be the first well dug in the city. The square where it sat was bordered by Tam City's richest shops and it was here, to Aeon's surprise, that Sena kept his new receiving room.

Aeon couldn't help wondering how a greenwife, who lived in the crooked back streets of the dregs could possibly afford to rent at the heart of the market. But she supposed it was none of her business.

It was early and the streets were full of rumbling carts, hurrying through the streets for the brief two hours a day during which they were permitted to deliver their loads. Most of the produce entering the city came by the huge variety of boats that could dock at any time. The apothecary was locked up, its windows tightly shuttered, but when Aeon slipped round the side of the building, she saw movement in the window of the back room. She crept up to the back door, lifting the latch and stepping quietly inside.

Beyond the doorway was a short passage, dark, narrow, and windowless. Aeon moved on carefully. She could hear voices in the distance, a rumble of muted noise. Light seeped out from under a door in front of her. She stepped up, pausing to listen.

"I can't tell you who is making this, not yet, but I can tell you that it's dangerous." It was Sena's voice, sounding tense and almost brittle.

"What does that mean?" A coolly cultured voice, definitely noble and oddly familiar.

"I don't know. I thought it was just contaminated, cut to go further but I was wrong. This has been deliberately compiled. It's killing people and that might be deliberate too."

"Killing simulacra, you mean." The noble's voice was sharp.

"I think someone is testing this on simulacra, looking to manipulate them in some way. But I doubt it will be used against the Makers' artificial life when it's done."

There was a sharp sigh. "More than a month we've been working on this. You have all the equipment you need here, and you still have nothing but superstition."

"I'm a greenwife, Tahl, not omniscient. Tahl…wait!" Sena's words rose in volume, and Aeon was aware of the sound of soft shod footprints a moment before the door was thrown open and she was pulled violently into the room.

The greenwife released her arm instantly, leaving her standing alone in the middle of the room, under the sharp gazes of Sena, two armed guards in imperial livery and a tall, broad shouldered woman with short, immaculately cut hair and a beautifully embroidered silk jerkin.

Aeon swallowed. Tahl a'Tam. She felt again the crawling sense of shame and guilt that she had felt on the night after Mara's funeral.

The princess eyes were wide, her face rapidly paling as she stared at Aeon. One hand fell to hilt of the sword she bore at her waist, even as she stumbled back a step or two. Her fingers were trembling.

"Mara!" she said.

Aeon flinched. "No," she said as softly as she could. "I'm not her."

"It's her simulacra, Tahl." Sena said quietly into the sudden silence.

"Her simulacra? Mother sent it back to its Maker be destroyed."

"It didn't take." Aeon said.

"But you can't. You can't walk around with my sister's face." There was anger now, it was growing in the Tahl's shaking voice, in her brown eyes. Aeon recognised that anger.

Aeon sighed. "I don't have much choice."

"I could have the guard take you back to your Maker. I could have them stand and watch as the deed was done.

How?" She glanced across at Sena as if for reassurance. "How dare they let her walk off like this, like my sister was nothing?"

"They didn't let me do anything. "Aeon snapped.

"Aeon was left for dead." Sena explained. "Naevus found her and brought her home."

Tahl swung towards him. "You condone this?"

Sena sighed, reaching out to lay a hand on Tahl's. "I know how you feel, but Aeon isn't her. It's just a face."

Tahl gave an incoherent cry and pulled back from Sena's touch, swearing profusely.

"There is no point in blaming Aeon for this," Sena said matter of factly.

Tahl glared. "You don't think this is suspicious?"

"Suspicious?"

"Aeon fails in her duty, Mara dies and now, somehow, Aeon escapes her own death to live on. Almost as if someone were rewarding her for..."

"Rewarding me for what?" Aeon could hear the coldness in her voice. She barely noticed how her hands curled into the fists by her side, but behind her the sound of steel rasping clear of sheaths filled the air.

"Aeon doesn't know anything." Sena sighed. "Leave it be."

Aeon didn't know whether to be offended at being so easily dismissed. Tahl waved towards the guards though and the swords were quietly sheathed.

"Here," Sena said soothingly. "Sit down. Aeon, you might as well sit too, I assume you came to ask me about the vial."

Aeon nodded and sank into a chair while Tahl glared at Sena and the greenwife stared blandly back.

"You heard what we were saying earlier." Sena said.

"Yes," said Aeon. "The contaminated split shots are being used on simulacra on purpose."

"That's more than likely."

Aeon could think of plenty of reasons why that might be useful. "But you don't know what they're meant to do."

Sena sighed. "I don't think they've got them to work yet."

"Makers are using rogue simulacra to test this solution because they think they won't be missed?"

Sena nodded.

Tahl looked back and forth between them, her face hard. "You think the Makers are planning something, Sena?"

"Or a faction of them, yes."

"What do you think they are planning?"

Sena's voice dropped low and cautious. "I don't know, they've killed several simulacra and a Maker's servant so far. I don't know how high they're setting their sights. But the Makers hold their mandate from the Empress herself. At the very least they're killing the Empire's citizens; at the worst its…"

Tahl swore again, this time very, very quietly. "Treason."

Sena nodded.

Aeon sat there in the comfortable surroundings of the greenwife's receiving room and thought of Talon's words from the night before. It wasn't only the Maker on Green Street that was selling contaminated split shots. It was her Maker too.

Tahl left soon after to report to the Empress. When Sena pointed out that she was banned from the palace, Tahl replied tartly that where there was a will there was a way and swept out. She passed Aeon with a hard look in her brown eyes. The guards, silent and watchful, followed in her wake.

Sena walked over to a store cupboard and started packing a leather bag. His long fingers were careful as he placed narrow wads of cotton between the clay jars to keep them from hitting each other. His green eyes glittered in the lamplight.

"How do you know Princess Tahl?" Aeon said at last.

Sena's fingers stilled and he looked up. "I could lie to you," he said.

"You could." Aeon acknowledged.

"She's my twin sister," he said, his smile more of a grimace.

Aeon stared at him. "Your sister!"

"My father was a minor noble, who had a brief fling with the Empress. Tahl was born a cherished daughter but I was both a son and a greenwife." He stared down at the box. "The Empress ordered the midwife to take me away and dispose of me. The woman gave me to her sister instead."

"Her sister?"

"She was also a greenwife. She fed me, clothed me, taught me her trade. I took over her receiving rooms when she died. I grew up in the dregs, a child of the rope bridges."

"But you know Tahl now?"

Sena grimaced. "She came and found me, five years ago. The midwife confessed on her deathbed."

"She pays for this room?"

"Just while we're looking into this business with the shots. She can hardly come and find me down in the dregs every time I have news."

No, Aeon supposed she couldn't.

Sena closed the bag. "I have to go," he said.

#

Sena had patients to see, so Aeon walked back to Swallow Street, thinking all the way about poison and changing faces and Solel a'Vari. The Maker's Apprentice was the scion of a noble house as the a' in his name indicated, short for *amrit*, an ancient designation of nobility. He had been raised in comfort in the bosom of his wealthy family until Maker Larch came for him. No one knew how a Maker chose his Apprentice, and each Maker had only one, but once you were chosen there was no denying the Maker's will.

Aeon remembered Solel as a nervous boy, his soft hands peeling the remnants of the chrysalis from her skin as she emerged fully grown into the world. She had thought of him as a friend, yet according to Talon, he was involved in the selling of contaminated shots. Was Maker Larch involved too? Or were they unwitting fools, targeted because they were personal Makers to the Empress?

Aeon pondered as she wondered back towards the dregs. It was a miserable afternoon; rain had begun to fall, misting the world in shades of grey and the wind was cold. Aeon pulled her cloak tight about her shoulders, drawing the hood up to shield her face from both the weather and the eyes of those she passed.

For a start, she could determine exactly who was selling the shots. By tradition neither Maker nor Apprentice went out in public unmasked. There was no way Talon could know which of the two Glint had bought from. She was sure whoever it was would take care to conceal their actions.

When Aeon reached Swallow Street, she found Sixfingers idling in the kitchen. Everyone else was out. It seemed the merchant's fears had been well founded; an attack had almost

killed Talon. Naevus and Roe had gone to help Glint bring
her home.

Aeon closed her eyes to the remembered pain of burning
brands, cold metal teeth against her skin, the rasp of breath
in her throat and blackness rising like the tide and suppressed
a shudder.

"I'm glad Roe is doing better," she said.

Sixfingers grunted. "It is good to have a distraction."

Aeon didn't need to ask how Roe was feeling. There was
still a hollowness inside her whenever she thought of Mara's
face, or laugh, or funeral. An emptiness she suspected would
never leave.

"What did the greenwife have to say?" Sixfingers asked,
changing the subject.

"Someone is using rogue simulacra to test an experimental
split shot. Sena can't tell what it does."

"Someone?"

"A Maker."

Sixfingers scowled. "Doesn't surprise me."

Aeon looked away. Her skin prickled every time she
considered that Solel or Maker Larch might be involved. They
had built her, fed her, cared for her and taught her. They
contracted her to the palace, to a life of luxury and status,
even if it was tied to her original. And weren't all simulacra
tied to their originals in the end? Well, maybe not rogues.

Aeon glanced across at Sixfingers. She was leaning back
in her chair, booted feet on the table. She was relaxed in her
body, loose limbed and serene, utterly sure of herself. Aeon
wasn't sure that she'd ever felt like that. She had always been
conscious that she wore a borrowed face, that her body was

someone else's body. She was a mere image, a copy, like a painting, or a statue. There was no 'self' only Mara and Mara's fetch.

"What is it really like to wear one body for so long?"

"I've forgotten what it is to be any other way. Before the captain I was in Glint and Talon's line of work, so I've worn a fair few forms over the years."

Over the years.

"How old are you?"

Sixfingers grinned. "Seventy-two. I'm the oldest here, by at least three decades."

"Seventy-two?"

Sixfingers grinned. "We don't age, Aeon, we don't get ill, we can repair most forms of damage and we look like real people." Her lips quirked. "A simulacra can get pretty far on that."

Aeon frowned. She'd never thought of all the things simulacra could do that originals could not. "That's why Makers send hunters after us, isn't it?"

Sixfingers nodded solemnly. "It's part of it. They're afraid of us rogues and they don't want the rest of the world to discover just how little control they really have."

Naevus, Talon, Glint and Roe came in shortly after. Talon was being carried by the others, who laid her down gently on the settle in the sitting room, wrapping a blanket about her shoulders. She was pale and looked utterly worn, dark shadows showing purple beneath her eyes. Glint, setting himself down beside her, looked almost as exhausted. There were marks of tears on his stiff face.

"The merchant paid us off," he said. "He fancies himself

safe now."

"Good." Roe said. "That attack was vicious, and you know Talon's not strong enough."

Glint sighed. "I know." His voice was low. "I really thought they'd go for the son. The merchant was always talking about how his son was set to take over the business after him. The girl barely left the house. I wouldn't have been surprised if no one knew she even existed."

"Well, someone obviously did." Naevus said sharply. "No doubt they thought her the easier target."

"Well, they were wrong, weren't they?" Glint said. His voice hard.

Naevus laid a soft hand on his shoulder. "Yes, child, they were wrong."

They scattered then. Naevus went to find a pillow and more blankets, so Glint could spend the night in the room with Talon. She had fallen asleep, her face hollow in the shadows, the marks of pain still obvious even in unconsciousness.

Roe, weaving with tiredness, was escorted upstairs by a concerned Sixfingers.

Aeon went into the kitchen to fetch her cloak. It wanted only a few hours until curfew; if she meant to creep into the Maker's District, spy on the house of her Maker and leave again, then she had better hurry. The city's folding bridges were pulled up just before curfew and not lowered again until the brother set, separating each district into its own little island. It was possible to scull or swim across, but you had to be careful, bridge guards spent the night watching out for just such manoeuvres.

"Where are you sneaking off to?" Naevus had come into

the kitchen. Their dark gaze was hard, assessing.

"I just need to check something."

"And where would you be doing this checking, may I ask?"

Aeon hesitated. "The Maker's District."

Naevus reached up, pulling down a grey cloak from a hook. "I'm coming with you."

Chapter Four

Naevus didn't say much, following in Aeon's wake like a shadow. With their slight build and nondescript appearance, tattered cloak and soft leather boots, they could have passed for anything from a child to an elder.

The horizon was still pink and gold from sunset, the clouds having parted just as the sun sank out of sight and neither the golden sister nor the pale brother had yet climbed into the sky. Aeon glanced north, taking comfort in the ethereal arch of the Dark Mother's Gate where it stretched glowing across the horizon against twilight's fall.

The city streets were still busy, bright with the bustle of people heading home or out to work. The industries of the Fabrication District were never idle, simply exchanging day shift for night shift with monotonous regularity.

The Fabrication District was connected by a regular ferry service to the pleasures of the Scarlet District where gambling dens, doxy houses and illegal markets offered delights that could not be matched by the respectability of the districts that fell skyward of the spine. Beyond that district the rope and rag bridges lead to the dubious streets of the dregs.

A steady stream of workers and off duty servants headed for the boats nightly. Not the city's nobles. They reached the Scarlet District via one of a series of folding bridges from the Market. Travelling by water only when they sought to return home from their lowly pleasures. The flash of a silk seal was enough to gain their craft passage along the city's straits long after curfew. It had always been one rule for the rich and another for the poor.

Walking against the crowd, Aeon led the way towards the Silvergate Bridge. Naevus glanced across at her every now and then but said nothing. They crossed into the district without any trouble and Aeon soon found herself back in familiar streets, looking for the blue door and her Maker's house.

Just as in Green Street, Aeon found a doorway across from an alley and the door of Maker Larch's workshop. She slipped into the heavy shadows left by the spreading branches of a landolen tree. Naevus sliding in beside her.

It wasn't until she stopped moving that Aeon realised how tight her muscles were. There was a bitter taste in her mouth and a sharp feeling in her stomach. She drew in a few breaths to calm herself. Her fingers were shaking.

Naevus laid a soft hand on her shoulder, clutching it tightly for a moment or two. The grip was hard and warm, and Aeon felt a little steadier. The street was quiet, empty. Most of the houses ablaze with light. Shutters open to flood the world. There were lights in her Maker's house too. Aeon watched the flicker of flame through the windows.

The back of the house was dark and still, thick with shadow. It smelt damp.

Aeon drew in another breath and for a moment she was

back there, wet wood against bare skin, dead flesh pressed against her. Fire blazing through her veins.

She pressed her lips tightly together – she would not be sick.

Naevus touched her shoulder again.

A figure was making its careful way up the street. It was trying to be inconspicuous, but its nervousness was obvious even at a distance. A hood was pulled low over its face, but Aeon caught a glimpse of bright silks beneath its cloak. It moved like a simulacra.

The figure stopped by the back door. It glanced around briefly, forcing Aeon to draw back into the shadows. Then it knocked once, paused, three times, paused, then twice.

It waited.

Aeon waited too, hardly daring to breathe.

Who would answer the door?

For a long moment nothing happened, and Aeon began to feel a creeping sense of relief.

Then the door at the back of her Maker's house swung open.

The servant Bleak stood in the doorway, peering out with his customary disgruntled face. The hooded figure murmured words too soft for Aeon to hear. Bleak scowled, nodded and pushed the door shut in the figure's face with a fine lack of manners.

Another wait.

Shorter this time.

When the door opened again, Solel stood in the archway. He was barefaced, smiling, his blue gaze warm and a blood red vial in his right hand.

Aeon swore under her breath and beside her Naevus shifted, murmuring something indiscernible. Aeon suspected it was meant to be comforting. She groped out blindly in the dark and felt Naevus's hand, warm and solid in her own.

#

So, Solel was involved. Talon hadn't been mistaken. He'd sold Glint a shot that had nearly killed him. He was experimenting on rogue simulacra; he was complicit in whatever plans were being carefully and painstakingly put together right now.

Aeon thought of nothing else on the long, dark walk back to Swallow Street. Naevus said nothing, moving like a shadow at Aeon's side. Though the street was much quieter now, the bridge guards gave them barely a glance as they ambled over the arch of the bridge. Most likely the guards assumed they were a pair of servants heading home before curfew, or wholesale runners, delivering goods in the district.

The streets of the city were still busy around the broad expanse of the market district with its flag stoned squares and cap stoned wells, not yet sealed for the night. Stalls still lined the boulevards and many of the shops were open, curfew was still an hour or two off, plenty of time for shopkeepers to lock up and send their staff scurrying home. Aeon and Naevus slipped through the crowd, Aeon noticed how easily Naevus moved and how nondescript they were among the whirling throng. If Naevus didn't want to be noticed - they weren't.

Aeon envied the nix's skill as she murmured apologies, stepping out of the way of hurrying multitudes, who brushed by without looking up. Goods were brought into the city through the Shipping District where ocean going ships tied up at the wharfs. But their loads were transferred onto smaller boats that moved easily beneath unfolded bridges. Their engines puffing faintly across the water, greenish copper scented smoke hanging in their wake. There wasn't a building in the city that didn't have a set of brick steps or small quay at its base, with iron rings buried into the walls, awaiting the mooring ropes of the carrier boats.

Aeon and Naevus crossed the spine and headed through the Scarlet District, towards the makeshift bridges of the dregs. Aeon was hungry; the sick feeling had faded from her stomach and she was looking forward to the warmth of the kitchen, a cup of hot khvā and maybe a long evening of conversation with Naevus and Sixfingers. Together they would decide what to do next. And maybe they could decide to do nothing. This was the palace's problem after all. The Empress was the one threatened by treason and she had a lot more resources than half a dozen rogue simulacra hiding from hunters in the back end of the city. Aeon wasn't Mara's fetch anymore; she wasn't anyone's fetch. This wasn't her problem.

Aeon was profoundly thankful to reach the ragged pier and the tall, thin shadow of home. The street was dark, there were no sunstone lamps here, in their delicate glass globes, as there were in the richer city districts. Here, the world was illuminated by the glow behind ill-fitting shutters, the glitter of stars and the gleam of the Gate. Shortly the sister would rise, round and bright and curfew would fall.

Aeon followed Naevus's soundless steps out along the pier.

The house was unshuttered and unlit. Were they all dormant? Maybe they were out. Surely Talon wasn't well enough to visit the Moth.

Naevus's steps slowed as they reached the end of the pier. The air smelt of damp and salt, the clicking song of night insects ringing loud in the stillness. A bat fluttered overhead. Laughter sounded from the house opposite and somewhere nearby a clear voice was singing an old, saltward tune.

Ahead of them, the house on Swallow Street was dark and still.

Aeon hesitated.

The front door stood ajar, darkness yawning.

"Naevus." Aeon could hear that her own voice was shaking.

"Quiet," Naevus murmured, silently drawing a long blade from their waist.

The nix moved silently over the threshold and Aeon followed, heart beating loud in her ears, her breath so tight in her chest that her ribs ached.

The door moved silently to let them in, not offering a whisper of noise. The hallway beyond showed only shadows and the dim bulk of gaping doors. Naevus headed for the kitchen.

It was at the back of the houses, overlooking the waters of the bay. Aeon supposed a lamp burning there might be invisible from the street. It was as dark as the rest of the house but there was movement. A rustling of cloth across the ground and what sounded like hard, gulping sobs.

Naevus stopped in the doorway, still holding the blade tight in their right hand, they flung out their left, tipping up the foci of their one sunstone lamp. Butter yellow light leapt into the room.

There was blood on the floor. For a moment in the sudden

glare it was so dark it looked black. Then colour flooded back to Aeon's eyes and she saw red, so much red. A tumble of flesh lay beside the table, curled into itself like an insect in a cocoon. Another body sprawled slack limbed beside the door, close enough that Aeon could bend down and touch it. Open eyes and a tumble of golden-brown curls. Glint.

Was the body by the table Talon?

Naevus had not moved, had not even lowered the blade. Aeon stepped passed the nix, crouching beside the still form.

Roe.

Sightless eyes stared back at Aeon, mouth open in a soundless scream. Someone had jammed a blade deep into the back of his skull; both spine and brains spilled out onto the dirt of the floor.

Aeon swallowed bile.

Another rustle.

Aeon stumbled past the table.

A cloaked figure was crouched on the floor in front of the fire.

Aeon let out a wordless cry and it turned.

The greenwife stared up at her. He was drenched in blood, his hands red to the elbow, his chest soaked. There were the tracks of tears and more blood smeared across his face.

Aeon started to tremble.

"Fingers is still alive, just." The words were a hoarse croak, as if he had already worn his voice away. Green light glowed faintly between his fingertips.

Aeon glanced passed the greenwife. Sixfingers lay in a spreading pool. Could you lose that much blood and still live? There was gaping wound in the back of her head, as if someone had aimed for the spine and missed. If she was still alive, they must have missed. Aeon did not look round to where Roe lay, warm to the touch but so still.

"What about Talon?"

Sena drew in a shaking breath and Aeon realised that it had been his sobs she'd heard in the dark. He shook his head. "On the settle in the other room. I don't think she even woke up."

Behind Aeon, Naevus started to swear, deep, hard, vicious words that went on and on rising windswept in the stillness. Aeon's legs started to shake and a moment later she was on the floor, trying to remember how to breathe.

All of them. All of them.

"What happened?"

"Blue lips and fingers," Sena said curtly. "They were dosed with fever-gas, they would have been helpless."

"Hunters. Has to be. That's a professional kill." Naevus's voice was hollow.

"We need to go." Sena glanced across at Aeon. "Can you help me with Fingers?"

Aeon hesitated. Trying not to see the way skin and flesh bulged from the side of Sixfingers head. "Should we move her?"

"No choice. We can't risk being there if the hunters come back. They could be watching the house right now." He glanced across at Naevus. "Nav, we have to go, we have to go now."

Naevus shook their head. Their face was so pale Aeon wouldn't have been surprised if they fainted right there. "We can't...." the words tumbled bloodless into the room. "We can't leave them."

Sena's face tightened. "We won't. Help me."

With Aeon's help, Sena manged to pull Sixfingers onto his back where she lolled, boneless. He staggered out of the kitchen into the darkened hallway and Aeon followed, towing Naevus along. The nix walked as if in a dream, eyes blinking but unfocused. Their hand in Aeon's was cold, their fingers trembling. Feeling like nothing so much as a metal automaton, favoured plaything of the imperial court, Aeon dragged Naevus out of the front door and over the rough boards of the pier.

There Sena stopped, staring blindly back towards the house, shoulders bowed under Sixfingers' weight.

Aeon felt a sudden lurch of horror and guilt. *What are we going to tell her when she wakes up? When she asks for Roe?*

"Sena?" Naevus's voice, it sounded distant as the stars.

Sena glanced across at the nix. "I'm going to burn them. Send them out in style. Let the Dark Mother see how precious they were, how…loved."

For a moment it seemed as if Naevus hadn't understood. Then they nodded.

Sena raised a hand, closing his eyes, face tight with concentration.

The spark was green. It skipped across the pier, leaving a streak of green flames in its wake, and slammed into the front door. Moments later a green fireball exploded out of a ground floor window.

He dropped his arm, his face going blank.

The house on Swallow Street burned, smoke billowing out over the water. The pilings of the pier caught in a moment, green flames racing along old warped wood. A wave of heat flashed against them, carried on a wind that hissed and fizzled. Then with a quiet groan and a sudden lurch the pier buckled, the pilings cracked and the house on Swallow Street tumbled down into the cold, dark waters of the bay.

Aeon suspected that if left to themselves, Sena and Naevus would have stood there watching the house burn long into the night, oblivious to the skies opening, and the deluge of rain that cascaded over the city. They both seemed to forget Sixfingers lying there on the mud-stained road, standing glassy-eyed before their blazing home.

Aeon managed to cut through their shock and grief with persistence and gentle words, dragging them from the conflagration that consumed both their sanctuary and their friends. She coerced them across the district, carrying Sixfingers' dead weight between them, to find a boatman to take them across the channel to the market. They avoided the bridge guard at the cost of the coins in Sena's pocket.

The city was silent, caught in the trap of curfew and they saw nobody as they limped their broken way across the sprawling flagged squares of the district. The apothecary was shuttered and dark. Aeon led the way down the alley to the back door without a word. She supposed they were lucky that curfew was far enough advanced for the guard to have given up scouring the streets from stragglers and returned to the guard houses that sat over the great bridge windlasses like a shell over a turtle.

Sena's bare little room was dark and cold but being there seemed to rouse him. Aeon and Naevus lay Sixfingers carefully on his treatment table while the greenwife lit a pair of oil lamps with a wave of his hand. For a moment, Aeon could have sworn his fingers glinted green. The heady scent of fish oil filled the room, but Aeon preferred it to the stench of blood that drenched all their clothes. On the table Sixfingers was so pale and still that Aeon felt a brief swell of panic. Maybe the fist was dead after all. She steadied herself with a thought - Sena would not have allowed them to carry a dead person halfway across the city.

The greenwife reappeared, bearing his leather bag, and pulled out bandages, vials of poppy juice, needles, and thread. Naevus, visibly shaking, had sunk down into a chair, and sat there staring blindly into the room. Their face was almost grey, and Aeon did not need to touch their skin to know that it would be clammy and cold.

"Sena." She only said his name softly, but he must have sensed something in her voice for he looked up, glanced across at Naevus and then, nodding abruptly, pointed across the room.

"Strong spirits, in the jug over there, they should help."

Aeon poured the nix a generous measure. The golden liquid smelt of sunlight and fire and Naevus coughed sharply as it went down, but it did seem to bring some colour back to their cheeks.

Dark eyes sought Aeon's own, wide with pain and loss. She reached out, not even certain why she did so, and drew an arm about Neavus' shoulder, holding tight while they shivered against her.

"They're all gone," the nix choked out at last. "All of them."

"Sixfingers is still here," Aeon prompted softly but she wasn't sure that Naevus heard her.

At last the nix fell dormant in the armchair, still shivering and pale. Aeon tucked a blanket about their shoulders and tried to pretend she did not see the tears on their pale, exhausted face.

She glanced across at Sena who had finished whatever he had been doing to Sixfingers and was bandaging her head. His face was hard, and Aeon would have missed the shared horror and grief if she had not been looking into his eyes.

"What do you think happened?" she said at last.

"I think that whatever bastard cursed the merchant's daughter, got angry when the curse rebounded on the worker and found out that Glint and Talon were rogues. Not so hard to persuade their Maker to send the hunters; he always was a bastard."

"You're sure it was hunters?"

Sena shrugged, sitting back in the chair that had been set beside the bed. He looked unutterably weary. "Who else cares about a few rogue simulacra living among the dregs of the city."

Who indeed?

Sena soon followed in Naevus's wake, falling asleep with his head pillowed on his arms, resting on the bed beside Sixfingers' still form, as if he sought to watch over her even in his sleep. Aeon stared down at the fist's silent body. How were they going to tell her that Roe was gone? How were they going to tell her about Glint and Talon, or explain that the house, their home, was lost forever?

She didn't mean to fall dormant, but weariness crept up on her, dark and cold and thick with the scent of smoke.

She woke first, sunlight falling through the unshuttered

windows and onto her face. It was nearly noon. She supposed they were lucky it was a rest day, and no one had come knocking – or if they had, they had gone unheard.

Aeon sat up, glancing about the small, crowded room. Neither Naevus nor Sena had moved but Sixfingers' might had shifted a little, her colour was better too and her breathing less laboured.

Suddenly Aeon didn't want to be there when she woke up, which probably made her a coward, but she didn't care. Her own grief was like a hollow inside her, an empty ruin, she couldn't face seeing that reflected back in Sixfingers' kind eyes. Not fresh and raw, the first opening of the wound.

Besides there was someone else who might be bothered by a group of rogue simulacra in the city. Someone who might have spotted that they were being watched or heard that someone was asking questions about poisonous split shots.

Aeon grabbed her cloak, pulling it round her shoulders, not caring that it was still damp, weighing heavy against her shoulders. There was someone she needed to see.

#

Aeon reached the cresting archway of the Silvergate bridge in the blaze of early afternoon. Beyond its broad, white stone parapet, the Maker's district shone. Everywhere there were spires and clock towers, copper and brass. There was the rumble of wheels and the distant green haze of firestone smoke. Unlit stone lamps glowed in cages of intricate silver which were etched with dreamlike designs. The walls of residences encircled the steep pitched roofs of bustling workshops. The district was breath-taking, the very opposite of the worn and soot stained fabrication district, because the Makers of the Clockwork City only created things that were perfect, perfect and beautiful.

Aeon didn't hesitate, she pulled her cloak tight about her, drew up the hood and headed out over the bridge once more into the place where she had been born.

#

Solel was a creature of habit and his lunches were invariably taken at The Three Gears, a coffeeshop on the corner from Ochre and Crimson Street. He could have eaten with the Maker in private of course, but Solel had told her once that he enjoyed having a little time to himself and the Gear's coffee was second to none.

"Sometimes even the best of places can feel a little claustrophobic."

The shop was small, but it did have a few tables in the back room. Aeon ducked through the low beamed door to enter and, glancing across, saw Solel seated in a corner. He was using a table knife on a plate of smoked fish and boiled greens in front of him, beside which sat a cup of spiced coffee. The scent of it filled the room pleasantly. Aeon recognised cinnamon, apple and cloves.

He didn't look round as she entered, seemingly engrossed in his meal. She relished his slight jump as she slid onto the bench beside him.

"I don't suppose they sell khvā."

He stiffened, drawing back. His eyes widened as her face

came into focus. The knife clattered to the tabletop.

"Don't tell me," Aeon said with an insincere smile. "You thought I was dead."

He swallowed and then shook his head. "You were gone, the door was open. You either crawled out or you were stolen. Not much point in stealing a dead body."

"Why didn't you try and find me?"

Solel shrugged. "You'd already proven useless. What would be the point in spending money getting you back."

Aeon kept her voice even. "What do you mean useless."

Solel's eyes narrowed. "Haven't you guessed it? We wanted to cleanse you so you could be imprinted with a new original, but it didn't take."

"You're lying. Fetches don't get cleansed and re-contracted. They only ever belong to one original, that's why we're so expensive."

Solel's lips twisted into a slow, sweet grin. "Is that a fact?"

Aeon felt a shiver of cold as it slid down her spine and into her belly. It was Solel's face, his smile, his soft, warm voice. But there was nothing familiar about him at all.

"So," she fought to keep her voice steady. "You sell fetches on multiple contracts, and you supply rogue simulacra with split shots, even though by law you should send hunters after them. And you send simulacra out as imagoes if it pays better."

Solel shrugged.

"And what about the bad shots, Solel? What about the experiments you're conducting on rogues in the dregs?"

"I have no idea what you're talking about."

"That's odd because I've talked to simulacra who have bought shots from you." Aeon narrowed her eyes. "Shots that nearly killed them."

She clenched her hands into fists and tried not to think of Talon, dead on the settle where she should have been recovering from a curse.

"Does Maker Larch know what you're doing?"

Solel stiffened, his face paling slightly. "Of course."

Aeon didn't need to hear the slight jump of his heartbeat to know that too was a lie.

"Maybe I'm talking to the wrong Maker then." Aeon said softly, leaning forward as if she feared being overheard.

Solel almost flinched. "Look," he said, drawing back, eyes wide. Aeon could practically smell his fear. "We can't talk here." The room was filling up with crafters from the district seeking hot tea and good food before they went back to the workshops. "But I do want to talk."

He pushed his plate back, the rest of the meal uneaten and slide a coin across the tabletop. He stood up and Aeon followed his movements, measure for measure.

"Lead the way," she said.

He headed for the door of the shop before turning away towards a side door. A crowd of people had walked in, several Makers or Apprentices in their masks. Aeon assumed he was trying to avoid them. The side door led out into an unlit alley, narrow brick walls reaching up towards a strip of blue sky. The air was filled with scent of damp and rot, the tang of brine that never faded wherever in the city you might be.

The alley wasn't empty.

Three figures stood in the shadows. Two were tall and clad in dark cloth and leathers, their bodies wrapped in hoods and cloaks. Aeon caught the gleam of silver at their waists.

The third stood between them, shorter, cloaked in green. Somehow Solel had slipped behind her, closing the side door with a soft, careful click.

Aeon stepped away from him, feeling her back stiffen.

"What is this?" she said, as if she didn't know.

She could almost feel Solel's shrug in the tense air.

The figure in the green cloak started forward just as sunlight darted into the alley and across their face. For one half blinded moment Aeon saw clean lines, soft brown skin, a tangle of curls beneath the peak of the hood and a pair of hard, brown eyes. She took a step back, a ragged kind of gasp falling from her mouth.

This wasn't true, what she was seeing, it couldn't be…

The blaze of light faded, and it was if she could see again. Her gaze moved from brown eyes, bright she suddenly realised with suppressed fury. She saw the strip of cloth that gagged the wide, hard mouth, the iron about soft wrists. The bruises that were just starting to show on the left side of an angular face. The line of a jaw purple and swollen.

Everything rocked back down.

This wasn't a betrayal – this was…

The world went black.

Chapter Five

Aeon woke with a foul taste in her mouth and a breath of panic sharp in her chest. There was pain in her wrists and ankles, a knot of pressure against her back. She opened her eyes, careful to not move any other part of her. She was sprawled across a metal table, hands and feet bound with buckled leather straps. An ache ran up her arms and into her shoulders. To her right was an expanse of flagged stone floor and a high-backed chair. Tahl was tied tightly there, her face pale, her body slumped against her bindings. In the bright lamplight that flooded the room, the bruises and cuts on the princess's face looked ugly.

The room was silent. But when she dared to lift her head at last, Aeon discovered that they were not alone. The two black cloaked figures stood, motionless as statues, one at each of the room's two doors.

Aeon ignored them and looked about her. Neat wooden shelves stacked with clay pots, wax sealed jars and delicate glass bottles glittered in the lamp light. A long, pockmarked table ran along one side of the room. Its surface blackened with charring burns and unnamed stains. The air was sharp with the acrid scents of alcohol and other chemical compounds.

Maker Larch's workshop.

The first time she had been but newly emerged from her chrysalis, still sticky-wet and weak at the knees, Solel had led her inside, sat her down and wrapped a blanket about her newly fledged body. She could not speak, could barely see, the dim lamplight blinding to her never-before opened eyes. He'd placed her first cup of khvā into her hand, guided it to her mouth and helped her drink.

Later she had stood in the centre of this room while Maker and Apprentice inked the intricate brands of a fetch across the fresh skin of her arms, a rolling scroll of green, red and gold. Clockwork skin. The brands were designed to protect her original, flinging a cursed attack back on the curse-worker. She'd tried not to scream while they worked over her for hours, sweating and swearing in the stifling heat of the room. By the end of it her throat had been sore from muffling her voice.

It was here that Solel had pressed down the plunger on her first shot of ichor, filling her veins with the blending of Maker secrets and Mara's blood so that she might take on the princess's face and form. A personal guard against the kind of attacks that plague all royalty. It was here that she had begun, and Aeon was suddenly terrified that here was where she was destined to end after all. She had already nearly ended here once.

Opposite, Tahl stirred and open her eyes. She made no sound, not even a gasp of pain, but her jaws were clenched tight and she was very pale.

"You're awake," she murmured.

"Shh!" Aeon gestured towards the figures by the door.

The princess shook her head. "Gear-corps," she said, wincing at the pain the movement clearly caused her. "The Apprentice ordered them to stop us from leaving not to report what we said or did."

Gear-corps. The most dangerous of all the Maker's creations, creatures without thought, voice or will of their own, they obeyed only the simplest commands. They were as invulnerable as a simulacra, and with a word they would destroy a city, slaughter an entire people, set fire to the world even. Thankfully they were rare and difficult to make. They were not grown in birthing pools or hatched from chrysalid; they were fashioned from the city's unclaimed dead, the forgotten, the abandoned and the lost. Built from lifeless flesh, they were undone and reassembled under a Maker's skill into creatures of clockwork, controlled by whoever spilt blood over their personal seal.

Aeon tried to swallow down her disgust. How could she have misjudged Solel so completely? She'd thought the Apprentice clever and gentle and kind when all the time he had been…this. A killer, a destroyer, steeped in foul plots and fouler magics.

She glanced across at the princess. "We have to find a way out of here," she said. Though she couldn't conceive how, there were no windows, only narrow grates along the upper walls to let in faint sunlight and fresh air, and brass-geared dead guarding the door.

Tahl smiled faintly. "I've been thinking that too, but I haven't yet been able to discover one."

Aeon gestured awkwardly towards Tahl's face with a jerk

of her head. "What did they want?"

"To know what I know and then to know who else knows it."

"Did you tell them?"

"Not yet but I suspect it's only a matter of time."

Aeon swore and Tahl grimaced, looking apologetic.

"It's not your fault," she said. She wondered, against a wave of nausea, if Solel had just been waiting for her to wake up and what methods he would employ to force her to talk.

"What are you doing here? Why were you in the alley?" A sudden lurch filled Aeon's throat.

Tahl looked away. "The Apprentice grabbed me on the way to the palace." She nodded to the two figures by the door. "Those two had a hand in it and another of the Apprentice's friends." She shuddered. "There was something really wrong with him."

"Wrong?"

"Yes, he was…" She stiffened, the words dying in her throat. Then she jerked, her whole body drawing up straight in the chair, as if she had been struck by lightning.

"Tahl?"

A cry fell from the princess's lips, dragged out between tightly clenched whiteness, followed by blood that was more black than red.

Aeon pulled against her own bonds, swearing when the leather dug into her wrists. It was strong.

"What's happening?" The words tumbled from Aeon's throat.

Tahl gasped, dragging in a terrible sucking breath. She was shaking, judders so hard they bore the force of a seizure. "I don't know," she managed to hiss through straining jaws.

Aeon knew. "It's a curse."

Tahl just looked at her.

She was fighting, Aeon could see that and doing better than she had a right to. But it was only a matter of time. The attack would break her in the end, tear her body, shatter her soul. Solel and his conspirators would make her theirs and then everything she knew, everything she'd seen or heard or felt would be theirs.

Aeon cast about herself frantically. She needed out of these straps. But there was nothing. A bare tabletop, the stone floor, the table beneath her.

The table.

She bent her knees and pushed hard against the metal, hauling on the straps at the same time. It was sturdy but she was a simulacra - and she was desperate.

She felt the edge of the cuff bite into the skin of wrist and ignored it. She felt the sharp stab of metal as the buckle bent, twisting along her arms. Skin broke and tore. But the leather cracked, the buckle snapped, and her left hand was free.

It was the action of a moment to unstrap herself from the table and jump down.

She glanced at her arms. She was bleeding freely; from her left arm it was a persistent gush. She frowned for a moment, slowing the fountain to a trickle by closing off the torn artery and tightening the flesh and muscle array around it. It would need treating in the next few hours, but it could wait for now.

She moved through the room, keeping a wary eye on the gear-corps. They had not moved, and she hoped, if she stayed away from the door, that they wouldn't interfere. They had their orders after all. She suppressed a snort. Unlimited power was useless if it couldn't perform the simplest actions on its own.

She didn't need to leave the room to find what she sought. There, on the bottom shelf was row after row of blood red vials – split shots. And here, in this drawer, syringes. She grabbed a vial, a syringe and headed for Tahl's chair.

The split shot was a risk, she had no way of knowing whether it was clean or not, but she didn't have time to purge and shoot up fresh ichor. A permanent change took anything up to an hour, she only had minutes.

She filled the syringe from the contents of the delicate glass vessel. As they were named, one vial, one shot.

Tahl was soaked in sweat and panting heavily, her eyes bright with pain. Her hands had twisted against her bindings and were dripping red. She couldn't seem to speak but a babble of noise, notes of pain and fear, fell from her open mouth.

"Hold on." Aeon said. She didn't know if the princess heard her.

Aeon slid the tip of the needle carefully into Tahl's arm, ignoring the way she jerked and fell back, panting. She drew back the plunger ever so slightly, then drew the needle out and shook the syringe, mixing the princess's blood with the shot.

Tahl tried to speak, though Aeon couldn't imagine how she could think through the pain of the curse that was hammering into her body, bending her bones, scouring her flesh. There was blood running from her eyes and ears now, more blood forcing its way out beneath her fingernails. The princess was running out of time.

She crouched down beside Tahl, gripping her arm gently for a moment. "I've trained for this," she said quietly.

Even though last time she had been forced to change faces, it had almost killed her.

Beneath her hand, Tahl's skin was cool and clammy, more like a corpse than living flesh.

Aeon lifted the syringe to her own arm.

Felt the moment as it had been a month ago, when Solel had injected the killing solution into her body. Only it hadn't killed her – and this wouldn't either.

She slipped the needle in and pushed the plunger down.

Fire ran through her veins, fire flared in her gut, burning and burning. She could feel tears on her face, hot as scalding water. The pain filled her mouth with the taste of blood. But she fought against it. She pushed it away, blocked the screaming ends of her nerves, shut off thought until there was only need and want and must.

She kept her eyes tight closed as she felt her body re-knit itself around her. She couldn't hold it up anymore and she fell. She thought for a moment she felt Tahl's bloody hand on hers and then – blackness rose to swallow her up.

#

He is handsome, don't you think? A pretty-made boy, mother calls him but then she's not above chasing a pretty face.

The princess stood on the stone balcony above the training ground watching as a group of young courtiers in vivid silks and practical leather paced each other with delicately drawn swords. Her dark eyes were bright, bright enough to rival the sun.

"Do you think he will be at the festivities tonight?"

"I'm sure he will, everyone will be there, Highness."

A deep, warm laugh and a hand on her shoulder. "Mara, I told you to call me Mara, remember? Come, we have better things to do that ogle at pretty young men, amusing as that might be."

"Yes, Mara."

Another laugh and a whirl of skirts, dark hair in a heavy braid snaking down her long, slim back.

"You know, if I'm going to impress young men, we should really get a little dance practice in."

"I'm sure being a princess is impressive enough – Mara."

A softer laugh this time, like a secret they shared. She reached out; her hand warm against Aeon's fingers. "Do you really think so? Come and dance with me, Aeon, you know I love nothing better than to dance with you."

#

The darkness receded like a tide, leaving light and awareness behind. Aeon felt cold stone against soft skin and heard the gasps of Tahl's pain, only a breath away. Without moving, Aeon reached out to interrogate the shapes and lines of the new body. Broad shoulders, a tapered waist, only slightly taller than Mara's. It had known physical training, but not recently. Strong hands, a skitter of verdigris down the first finger on the left.

She raised her head and looked into the face of her original.

Wide, eyes, brown as topaz, stared back.

Her mouth was dry with foulness and her throat ached.

That face was her face now, that body her body.

For a moment she felt a pang of grief. Her mind full of Mara's cool paleness, her dark gaze and the way her lips curved when she smiled.

And then the curse hit her.

It was more than just pain, it was blackness, thick as smoke or ink. A twining force that battered against Aeon, hard enough to send her staggering backwards.

Tahl reached out, hand warm against Aeon's fingers. Her touch was strong, steadying, just as her sister's had been.

Aeon pushed herself forward, squaring her shoulders, standing between her original and the curse that boiled through the room.

Beneath the sleeves of her shirt, Aeon's body reacted. She had been worried about her lack of brands but that didn't seem to matter once a curse was active. She felt the searing of red-hot metal as it wormed its way up to the surface of her skin and burst out. Disks of brass and gold, of copper and bronze unfolded down her arms from shoulder to wrist. They were curved and corrugated with metal teeth like cogs or gears. Each circle fitting into the next as it pushed through Aeon's flesh, spilling blood down her new skin.

The cogs hummed softly as they fitted into place. They would be warm to the touch and when Aeon glanced down, she saw that her shirt was slick with blood. But she could feel their strength as they drew the curse down towards her. The humming grew louder, filling her ears, vibrating through the room as the cogs turned. Aeon could feel the pressure of the teeth as they moved against her body, increment by increment. She drew in a ragged breath.

Her clockwork skin pulsed.

The curse convulsed, shuddering as it struck the brass and gold that gleamed along Aeon's arms. It struck and rebounded, spinning up into the air. Aeon wondered if anyone else could see what she saw. Was the curse visible to the silent gear-corps at door? Could Tahl see the thing that was attacking her as she shivered and cried out, hunched over in pain? Or was the darkness Aeon's alone.

She raised her arms, holding them crossed like shields before her and pushed. She felt her body bend, threaten to break. She heard the creak of gears, the whirl of cogs as metal moved across her skin. She was part soft, fleshy body, part Maker's construct.

Light was rising in her, through her. Brilliant as the sun, golden as flames. It flared out, smashing into the curse and sending it reeling.

Aeon fell to her knees, trembling with effort. Her body flooded with pain.

The curse stuttered once, twice and, between one blink and the next, it was gone.

Aeon collapsed on her hands and knees, dragging great gasps of air into her lungs and thought she heard, off in the distance beyond the room, a bright and startled cry of pain.

The curse-worker receiving their own curse thrown back at them, twofold.

Aeon wanted to feel some kind of relief, some sense of triumph but all she felt was the bitter, grinding pain of clockwork against clockwork as brass and copper, green and gold disappeared back beneath her skin.

When Aeon looked up, she realised that the princess was staring at her, wide eyed. Almost as if she was afraid.

"I didn't know."

Aeon frowned, struggling to sit up. Her whole body was

shaking, and her mouth was dry. "Didn't know what?"

"I didn't know that when they said simulacra were made as much as grown, they meant it."

Aeon looked away, her face suddenly hot. Her jerkin and shirt were drenched in blood, but she could feel that riven flesh had closed over, her arms were as smooth as if they had never been broken.

"What was that?" Tahl said after a pause, during which Aeon managed to pull herself to her feet, though she was none too steady. She turned to look at the princess and realised that she had managed to rid herself of her own restraints. She stood a step away, brown eyes warm in the dim light. Her face was thin and worn, bruised and bloody.

"That was my escapement." Aeon felt the smile that tilted her lips, it was a half-smile, crooked and hesitant. Was that how the princess smiled? "It allows me to fight curses."

Tahl was still eyeing her warily. "It looked painful," she said.

"It is."

"Well, if it helps at all, I think you managed to hurt the curse-worker." Tahl added after a moment.

"I can't destroy a curse." Aeon said, "Just turn it back on the one who cast it."

Tahl's answering smile was grim. "Someone will have noticed your…defence. We need to get out of here."

"With pleasure." Aeon gestured to the gear-corps at the doors. "But what about them?"

Tahl's face hardened. "Leave them to me."

She stepped past Aeon, walking to the corner of the room where several long metal poles leaned against the wall. Their tips were pointed and sharp, used to free chrysalides from the ceiling of the birthing house once the simulacra inside started struggling to climb out. Tahl hefted the pole as if testing its weight.

"Which door?" she said.

Aeon blinked. "What?"

"Which door leads us out of this place?"

The door on the far side of the room lead to the inner corridors of the house. The door nearest them to a narrow, brick passage and beyond to the wide, airy space of the birthing house.

"That way," Aeon said, gesturing.

Tahl nodded.

"Get ready to run."

The princess, clearly battered and exhausted, readied herself, holding the pole like a lance in her strong hands.

Aeon wanted to call out a warning, wanted to remind her of what gear-corps were, of what they would do to obey their master's word. But before the words could leave her mouth the gear-corpse by the door moved. It turned to meet Tahl's approach; its body was slow but had a simulacra's grace. A blade hissed from its sheath and it pushed back the hood from its head. The room seemed to grow darker as Aeon watched, but it was only that its shadow blocked the lamp light.

It was taller than Tahl, its corpse flesh white, its eyes empty. Aeon could see the lines and pools of golden metal which filled in the pits and scars of killing wounds. More metal in shades of copper and brass figured in the mesh of gears and wires that were buried in the right side of the gear-corpse's head where the skull had been cut away, exposing the brain.

Like Aeon's escapement the clockwork protected the gear-corpse from a death blow to the head. The cogs and meshed wires were plated, their core, like the core of all Makers' creations, was made of ossium, the Maker's metal.

Tahl hefted the pole, her face grim.

Aeon's body tensed. *It's going to kill her.*

Tahl leaned forward ever so slightly before launching herself, aiming the pole straight at the gear-corpse.

It never even tried to move. The sharped end of the pole caught it square in the middle, ramming through under the weight and speed of the princess's attack, pinning it to the brick wall beside the door.

Tahl fell on her knees, panting with effort, as the gear-corpse tugged at the metal piercing its body, arms and legs waving impotently in the air. Aeon was reminded of nothing so much as a butterfly newly pinned on a collectors' board. The corpse on the other side of the room hadn't even looked round.

Tahl staggered to her feet. "We should go."

Aeon shot the bolt on the door, heaving it open and, with the princess a step behind, they entered the dark.

#

The passage that led between the workshop and the birthing house was short, dark and cold. The floor was rough packed dirt, the walls a curve of stained red brick. It was wide enough that a row of wood and iron tables stood along one side.

They were heavy and Aeon strained her shoulders as she shoved one in front of the door. She daren't guess how long the gear-corpse might remain pinned to the wall; what if Solel returned? Or the curse-worker seeking revenge? The table wouldn't slow them down forever, but it would help. There were bolts on this side of the door and she shot them to.

"Aeon." The princess's voice sounded strange, bouncing and echoing in the brick room. When she turned Aeon saw why.

Not all the tables were empty. A little further down the passage there were two figures draped in pale cotton sheets. As Aeon approached, Tahl lifted the first cloth.

It was Fallow, looking almost as he had the last time she saw him, dead on the floor of the kitchen. His empty eyes stared up at the ceiling, the fare for his soul-journey gone. Aeon reached out as if to touch his face and felt a resistance that stung and crackled beneath her fingers. Solel was keeping him like this: dead but unchanging. Why was he here? And whose ashes were in the urn that had burnt away in the blaze that consumed the bodies of his friends?

She could think of one reason why Solel might want the body of a rogue simulacra who died of a split shot.

She pulled aside the other sheet. Another simulacra, this one unknown to her, though she could guess how she had died. The hollow sound of pounding on the door behind them echoed through the confined space.

Aeon shook herself. "Come on," she said.

They hurried from the passage, passing through the still shadows of the birthing house with its row of giant cauldrons, and further on along the marble-tiled edges of the birthing pool, its water viscous and opaque.

They almost made it.

The birthing house opened out onto the yard with its high brick wall and sturdy double doors. Aeon avoided looking at the two-wheeled long barrow that stood on the far side of the yard. She had assumed the dead bodies piled there the night Aeon was left for dead, had been gathered to feed the pool. But maybe they were there for another reason. Perhaps they were there to furnish a gear-corpse's raw flesh.

Was there nothing vile that Solel did not have a hand in?

How much could a mere apprentice do without their master's consent?

Maker Larch had to be involved – didn't he?

They crossed the yard. The double doors that led to the alley outside were barred, not locked, but the bar was heavy, crafted from thick, old oak and strengthened by Maker cunning.

As if they feared attack. As if they had something to hide.

Together Aeon and Tahl grabbed the bar and heaved, lifting it clumsily from its iron brackets. The sound of booted feet in the yard behind them sent the bar thudding back into place and they both turned. Aeon pressed herself against the door. Tahl's eyes narrowed.

Maker Larch stood in the doorway of the birthing house. He wore his Maker's mask, bronze, shaped into the intricate layers of larch cones and a stylisation of soft-tipped needles. It covered his face from hairline to cheek and shadowed his eyes.

Aeon froze, suddenly terrified by the weight of that dark gaze. She had told herself it was all Solel's fault, that the Apprentice had betrayed both her and his master. She'd been wrong.

Her Maker smiled.

"I thought this was all Solel, I thought it was him." Aeon's throat was tight. "But it wasn't was it? It was you. Solel was just your errand boy."

Maker Larch raised his hand and ripped the mask from his head.

Solel stared back at her. His face was dark with anger.

Aeon went cold. "Where's the Maker?"

"I'm the Maker now," he said.

And suddenly, terribly, Aeon understood; Master Larch was dead. How long ago had Solel killed him? Had he died as soon as Solel brought her back to the house? Aeon's gaze slid back to the cart across the yard. Had the Maker's body lain beside her in the cold darkness?

Her stomach clenched.

Solel stepped forward. At his back, silent as the dead, three cloaked figures moved in unison.

Three.

Mothers, could they beat those odds?

Gear-corps were not curses. Aeon wasn't designed to fight them, and it was plain that Tahl was both exhausted and hurt.

Aeon pulled herself away from wall, clenching her fists.

It wasn't as if she had a choice.

Solel walked into the yard, his arms outspread, a half-smile spread across his pleasant face. "You've surprised me, I admit it." His gaze slid round to Tahl. "From what I'd heard about you, I wasn't expecting this much of a fight."

Tahl swore.

"And I wasn't expecting you to be up and walking around." His gaze had swung back to Aeon.

She shrugged.

"But there is nowhere you can go now." He sighed. "Why don't you come inside, and we can talk."

"I'm not going anywhere" Aeon did not move, even as the back of her neck prickled with rising fear. "Why did you take Tahl?"

"I had to stop her spreading those spiteful tales." Solel smiled nastily. "She was clearly desperate for her mother to hear them."

"That's Her Sacred Majesty, to you, Apprentice," Tahl hissed, her face full of a tight and hard-held fury. Aeon put a hand on her arm, seeking to steady her. If the princess rushed Solel here his gear-corps would take her apart.

Tahl drew back from Aeon's touch but seemed to catch a hold of herself. She relaxed slightly, though the fierceness was still visible in her face.

Aeon turned back to Solel. "And why did you take me?"

He sighed, his expression softening. "You're different, Aeon."

Aeon shook her head. "No, I'm not."

Solel moved forward, the warmth never leaving his face. "Come inside, let me explain."

Aeon stiffened, opening her mouth to refuse. The nearest gear-corpse turned towards her with blank, patient eyes and Aeon clenched her teeth, feeling the edges of the escapement beneath her skin, present but inert.

Tahl tensed at Aeon's side, her expression suddenly wary. Her long brown fingers flexed open and closed. They had no weapons, either on them or within reach. The door was hard against their back. They had nowhere to go.

We are going to end here.

Or rather Aeon was hideously afraid that Tahl would end. Aeon would be taken, strapped back on that table, helpless and alone.

"I'm not going anywhere with you." Tahl's voice thrummed with tension. The faint lilt of it reminded Aeon, just for a moment, of Mara.

"I'm afraid you're wrong," Solel said, almost regretfully, as his gear-corps stepped forward.

Aeon drew in her breath, raised her hands, ready to fight with her body if she had nothing else. Maybe she was facing her end, but she would choose that over giving Solel anything he wanted.

Tahl shifted her weight, sinking into a crouch.

The double doors behind them exploded open.

Splinters spun through the air as the doors slammed into brick, sending up clouds of dust and debris. Tahl was on her knees, one hand clutching her side. Blood, red as cherries, slid through her fingers. Aeon crouched beside her, pulling her to her feet and dragging her back from the door. A moment later another pair of hands were holding the princess up and Aeon was gazing into a grim smile and a pair of sharp, unflinching eyes.

Naevus.

Shaking, head ringing, Aeon looked past the nix. Sena was standing in the shattered doorway. His hair spilled around his head, his cloak streaming out in a wind that seemed to be his alone. His hands glowed with green fire.

Aeon swore. Naevus got Tahl's arm over their shoulder and began dragging the princess towards the alley beyond the Maker's courtyard. Aeon, desperately trying not to dislodge

Tahl's hand from her side, followed. The princess was alarmingly pale.

Sena was floating rather than walking as he moved into the yard.

Aeon risked a glimpse back. Solel was staring at the greenwife in shocked horror. Aeon had the sudden cheerful thought that he might faint away then and there. Instead he drew on a cord around his neck, pulling out a seal. Brass forged and etched. The gear-corps turned as one towards the greenwife.

"Come on," Naevus hissed. "We have to go."

"What about Sena? He can't beat three gear-corps on his own!"

Naevus raised an eyebrow." You don't think so? He told me to get you two out and he told me to run, and that's what I intend to do. Now, come on!"

Naevus couldn't carry the princess alone. Aeon scowled, turning her back on the yard, as Sena raised burning hands and wildfire crackled in the air.

Tahl was stumbling and breathing heavily as they left the yard and hurried down the alley.

"Where are we going." Aeon hissed.

"This way." Naevus led the way, their hands tight on Tahl's arm. Through the failing light the alley wound on, running parallel to the main streets, through hidden courts full of servant's children, outdoor privies, and bakehouses.

The passageway with its high, brick walls began to slope downwards, and Aeon knew they were heading for the water.

The mooring post was set just beyond a small square complete with a community well. The boat was small, little more than skiff, with a lever-wound, clockwork engine attached at the stern. Better than that, Sixfingers sat beside the tiller. She was pale, her face tight with tension and grief. But she was there, and Aeon was profoundly grateful.

"Here." Aeon called, drawing the princess's hand from around her shoulder. "Take her."

Sixfingers left the boat, accepting Tahl's weight as if it was a gift. And before she could think Aeon was running back the way she had come.

She couldn't leave Sena alone with the gear-corps. Their touch could null a greenwife's power. It was a side-effect of their nature that Era maintained was proof they were the Dark Mother's children. Aeon had always wondered what that made simulacra.

She reached the broken door, pausing to peer cautiously into the yard. The air tasted acrid and smelled like gunpowder. It sparked against her tongue.

Wildfire, green as sea glass burst out across the enclosed space, impossibly bright. It picked a gear-corpse up as if it were a doll and flung it across the yard into the far wall. Gold veins split apart, tearing flesh from bones as the corpse fell apart.

Maybe Naevus was right; maybe Sena didn't need help.

Sena glanced up at Solel, grinning wryly. "It seems the Green Mother finds your toy's existence offensive," he said.

Solel did not answer his smile. He raised the seal again.

The second gear-corpse fared no better than the first, crumpling to the ground when green lightning took its head half off its shoulders.

"She's been quite clear with me; she really doesn't like

them." Sena spoke matter of factly, as if it was a usual thing to speak with a goddess. Perhaps it was when you were a prosopopoeia of the Green Mother.

Aeon glanced down at the shattered gear-corps. Blank eyes stared back. One corpse lay with its face turned away. The other, broken-necked, left arm detached at the shoulder, right leg unmade at the knee, stared into Aeon's face as if it was about to speak. It's face, behind the dead white skin, was only a face. It could have belonged to anyone: original; simulacra.

Aeon had a sudden urge to lean over and close its eyes.

Roe and Glint had looked like that, lying in the kitchen, blood on their soft skin. Silent faces turned up the ceiling. Roe and Glint had looked like that after someone drove a blade into the back of their necks, severing the spine from the skull.

Aeon swallowed down rising bile.

There was one cloaked figure left, only this one was different. It moved more like a simulacra than the dead. And for a moment it seemed to hesitate, as if reluctant to obey Solel's command.

The wildfire sizzled against Sena's fingers and went out. "That is not a gear-corpse."

"No," Solel admitted. "It's something new, unique. A living mind under a seal's command. I call it a thrall."

The thrall began moving slowly towards them, stalking them. It moved like a predator and Aeon caught a glimpse of sharpened steel beneath its cloak.

"Controlling the minds of originals is illegal." She said, her voice thready in the open space. Sena jumped; clearly, he had not realised she was behind him.

Solel shrugged. "Illegal doesn't mean wrong."

Aeon stared back at Solel; at the boy she had known, who had grown into a killer.

"You know this is wrong."

Solel shrugged easily, his thumb rubbing over the seal round his neck. A seal Aeon now realised controlled, not the gear-corps, but this new construction. In response the thrall crouched, ready to spring. It was tall and slim, with the broad shoulders and ready stance of a sword fighter.

"It doesn't have to be this way," Solel said. "The greenwife can go, your rogue friends too." His blue gaze bored into Aeon's face. "I just want you."

"Why?"

"I thought I had failed," he said simply. "I was wrong."

Aeon hesitated. She opened her mouth to agree. If it meant Naevus, Sixfingers, Tahl, even Sena were safe then it would be worth it.

The green of wildfire sparked once more between Sena's fingers. He lashed out, breaking apart the night. Solel was flung to the floor, his hands clutching at his throat. The greenwife grabbed Aeon's had and shouted. "Run!"

Chapter Six

When Aeon and Sena reached the boat, they found Tahl lying at the bottom, beside a bucket of niski offerings but in relative shelter. The mooring was already untied, held in place by Naevus's hand on the rope. As soon as Aeon and the greenwife tumbled on board, the nix loosened their hold and the boat lurched away from the quay.

Gasping for breath, Sena climbed in beside his sister. There were stains on his clothes, rivulets of what looked like tar, thick and viscous as purging fluid. Gear-corpse blood.

Aeon crouched in the stern, watching in silence as Sixfingers released the gin-brake and the boat slid out into the currents of the canal. Mist was falling, drowning the world in ghosts. Sena bent over Tahl, his face frowning, green eyes glowing in the gleam of the streetlamps they passed.

"Is she alright?" Aeon's voice sounded faint to her own ears, shaky as a child's.

"She will be." The greenwife's words were curt. He sounded exhausted.

Now was not the time to talk.

Aeon leaned back and closed her eyes, listening to the faint *phut phut phut* of the boat's engine as Sixfingers stirred them away, into the darkness.

#

"Where are we going?" It was Naevus, speaking for the first time in what felt like hours, though Aeon had heard no bell toll.

"That depends," Tahl said quietly. "Who are you?" She was sitting up, still pale, her side neatly bandaged, a cloak wrapped about her shoulders.

"They're my friends," Sena said, his voice uncompromising. "Solel killed their family. They want to help."

For a moment Tahl considered and then she said, "We're going to my house."

"Won't Solel and his…creatures be expecting that?" Aeon's mouth tasted bitter and she couldn't seem to stop shaking.

"They took me from the Market District. I doubt they know where I live. It's not commonly put about."

"Are you sure?" Sixfingers murmured.

Tahl's wide mouth quirked upwards. "Do you have a better idea?"

Sixfingers turned the little boat, guiding it under a nearby bridge and headed towards the nobles' district, known as the Tens.

"How did you know to come and find us?" Aeon asked into the silence.

Sena who had been staring down at his tar-slicked, bloodstained hands looked up. "Sixfingers woke up, said that it wasn't hunters at the house but Solel. They were looking for you." He hesitated. "Why do you look like my sister?"

Aeon shifted uncomfortably on the hard seat. "Solel set a curse-worker on her, tried to force her to tell him who else knew about the plan. It was the only way I could protect her. I used a split shot."

It would wear off.

Sena glanced across at his twin, who smiled wanly. Then back at Aeon, his face grave.

"Thank you," he said.

"She was the one who didn't break when Solel tried other means of persuasion."

Tahl made a face and spat into the canal water. The greenwife eyed his sister warily until she smiled again, more broadly this time.

The princess turned to Aeon. "I never wanted a fetch. I never thought I was important enough. Ninth princess out of nine. But I know how much Mara cared for you." Tahl's gaze grew more meaningful still. "I know how much you cared for her. Thank you."

Aeon felt herself flush, and turned her head away, looking out over the cool shadows of the water. "She was my original."

#

The boat glided up to one of several mooring stations along the edge of the Tens District. Tahl's house wasn't far from the water but then nothing in the city was. Curfew had yet to fall, the sister riding high and golden. The brother had yet to rise but he wouldn't be long. The Dark Mother's Gate was a cool arc, scattered with runs of moving cloud.

"We should get inside," Naevus said.

Tahl lead the way. As a group they moved quietly through the district, with curfew so close, the streets were largely deserted.

"What if Solel does know where you live?" Aeon asked tentatively, remembering the speed and fury of the gear-corps' attack. Sena's hands glowing with wildfire as he drifted through the air.

Tahl snorted. "I'm not devoid of protection," she said.

"Your protection didn't help you this time," Sena pointed out, rather testily.

Tahl had the grace to look embarrassed even as she scowled at her brother. "I wasn't expecting to be attacked on a visit to our mother."

The greenwife caught and held her gaze, his face dark with meaning

Tahl looked away first. "We're here," she said.

The building looked much like the residence of any wealthy noble. Expensive materials all used in tasteful and minimal ways. In many ways it wasn't much different from the Maker's house.

On their entrance, Tahl was met by a flurry of worried servants and hard-eyed men in black whose blades were worn. They looked as if they could deal with anything except a gear-corpse attack and Aeon fervently hoped that Solel had none of the foul things left.

When the others asked how he had managed to survive the yard, Sena simply said it was by the Mother's Grace, and that the Green Mother abhorred the use of the dead in such a manner.

Aeon wondered if it was the Mother's Grace that had drawn down the wind and filled Sena's hands with blazing wildfire. Had the greenwife simply prayed and been answered? Like everyone in the Empire, Aeon gathered at temple on feast days and left offerings on shrines but Sena had been born with the ability to speak directly to his Mother. She had never quite realised what that meant before.

Tahl's servants were efficient and quietly deferential, betraying by not so much as a glance their true thoughts on the rag-tag group that stumbled through their doors, bloodstained, bruised and filthy. Turns in the marble bath house and clean clothes were swiftly organised and before Aeon was really sure of anything, she found herself sitting in a soft bed under fine sheets and an embroidered silk quilt, in one of the ground floor guest bedrooms.

A stone lamp burned on a small table by the bed, warming the room with its golden light. Aeon found it comforting. She was too tired to think or worry or wonder about Solel or his plans. She lay back and closed her eyes.

Despite her exhaustion, or perhaps because of it, dormancy eluded her for a long while. Fear and horror and grief tangled themselves up in her head and every time she closed her eyes, she saw Glint and Roe lying dead on the floor. She saw the gear-corpse's hand on Tahl's unprotected neck, she felt the cold flesh of the dead pressed against her own. The darkness, when it did come, was very welcome.

She rose to the light of early morning.

Sometime during the night, Princess Tahl had faded from Aeon's face and body, leaving Mara's familiar features behind. Aeon stared at those dark eyes, that wry smile, in the mirror.

Breakfast was a quiet affair.

Tahl, still battered and bruised from the night before, carved into her fish as if she were eager for blood and Sena watched her with concern in his green eyes. Naevus seemed tired, as tired as Aeon felt and though no one mentioned it, the room felt too quiet, too still, as if it missed people who had never been there. Ghosts seemed to shadow them now. Aeon half expected to hear Roe's laugh, the scatter of rapid footsteps and the banging door that meant Glint and Talon were home. Even Fallow's bright invitation to fill a mug and pull up a chair.

When everyone had finished, Tahl invited them into the library.

There, among towering shelves full of beautifully bound books, they pulled up chairs and began a council of war.

"Well," Tahl said at last. "What do we do now?"

Sena frowned, glancing around the group.

"Solel wanted information from Tahl." His green gaze settled on Aeon. "But the originals who came to our house were looking for you."

Aeon flinched and Naevus laid a cool hand on her shoulder. "We're not blaming you."

"Really?" Aeon said.

"Really," Sixfingers growled, though she did not meet Aeon's gaze.

Sunlight fell through the tall windows; it set dust motes dancing in the air.

"Solel said I was different," Aeon murmured.

"Different how?" Naevus' tone was sharp.

"I've been thinking about that. Could one of you check

something for me?"

Sena and Naevus both nodded.

Aeon stood. Her legs were shaking, her hands cold and clammy. She passed her hands under the thick weight of her hair.

"I need you to check my seal," she said, wondering if her voice sounded as thin to the rest of the room as it did to her.

"What are we looking for?" Naevus asked evenly.

"You're looking to see if it's there."

Different Makers placed their seals on different parts of the body, shoulder, chest, the soles of the feet. Maker Larch placed his at the nape of the neck. Aeon could probably feel for it with the tips of her fingers. It was a slightly raised surface and cold to the touch, embossed ivory and gold. But she wanted to be sure.

"Well?" she spoke into the silence of a room which, even with the presence of the sunlight seemed suddenly cold.

"You know what we're going to say," Naevus answered." You've already guessed. It's gone."

Aeon glanced across at Sixfingers. "Where were Roe and Fallow's seals?"

Sixfingers expression was stiff. "On their right shoulders."

Aeon had seen the shoulder of Fallow's corpse where it lay in the tunnel at the back of the birthing house. There had been no seal.

"That's why Solel wanted me. They already put that stuff inside me, and I survived. I'm proof that it works."

Sena shuddered and Sixfingers swore softly under her breath.

"But what exactly does it do?" Tahl demanded." What are

they planning?"

Sixfingers swore again and Sena murmured soothingly to his sister.

Aeon closed her eyes.

The Maker's seals were one of the earliest laws pertaining to simulacra. It was illegal to attempt to pass those built by the Makers off as real people. They were useful, they were intriguing, they were expensive, but they were built things, crafted of magic and clockwork. Aeon had never felt like anything else. The seals were there, plain to see if you cared to look, right shoulder, the sole of the left foot, the nape of the neck. Your Maker's seal was like a mark of approval, a brag – *I made this*. Each one worked in perfect, flawless gold. You could feel them beneath your fingers, slightly raised against the smooth warmth of borrowed flesh.

And now the Makers were trying to change all that, trying to escape the ties of law, for what? Power? Wealth? Just because they could? The Makers had created the folding bridges of the Tamyin Empire. They had designed the bottomless wells that watered the city and built the sea defences that protected it from the ravages of winter storms. Maybe, to them, this was just the next challenge. Creating artificial life that was indistinguishable from the real thing.

Aeon's contract demanded that she be ended when her service was no longer required. Was that why Solel had used a split shot on her, because it would cost him nothing? Or was there some other reason?

Aeon opened her eyes.

"My brands!"

Everyone looked at her.

"Without my brands or my seal, I'm an identical copy. There is no way to tell me apart from an original."

Her escapement was still there, beneath her skin, edges of gold and bronze, but only she could feel it. To the touch her arms were pale, soft, and smooth.

"But where does that lead?" Sixfingers said.

"They're planning to use it on someone just like you. That explains why they wanted to know who else I'd spoken to." Tahl's voice was shaking.

Sena's expression was guarded. "I don't understand."

"They're going to use it on a fetch belonging to the Imperial Family." Tahl's tone was dark with horror. "They're going to use it on my mother."

A sensation like iced bronze ran down Aeon's spine.

Tahl swore, her voice tight and hard.

"Tahl?" Sena sounded worried.

"What day is it?"

"Catra Dal," Naevus said quietly.

The princess turned wildly to Aeon. "Solel, he was an Apprentice but he's a Maker now, right? He was wearing Maker Larch's mask."

Aeon nodded.

Tahl glanced between them all, her face pale. "Maker Larch has an evening appointment with my mother, every Catra Dal."

Sixfingers sucked in a sharp breath. "You mean tonight."

"Are you sure?" Sena said, ever cautious.

"Yes," Tahl replied firmly.

For a gambler, fop and skirt chaser, she was surprisingly steady when she needed to be. "Solel is planning to replace my mother, our mother."

"But why?" Sena exclaimed, his voice shaking.

Tahl sighed. "The Makers want to make and sell gear-corps. They have for a long time." The princess shifted uncomfortably in her seat. "And rumour says its more than just gear-corpses. A new invention, something more vicious, more dangerous than the walking dead."

Aeon thought of the courtyard, of the seal about Solel's neck. *The thrall.*

Naevus leaned forward, their narrow face eager and sharp. "How do you know all this?"

Tahl shrugged carefully. "Mara told me," she said.

"Mara?" Her voice was so quiet, Aeon was surprised anyone heard her. She could barely hear herself but then her ears had started buzzing and the beat of her own heart was thudding in her ears.

"She was investigating the rumours." Tahl smiled ruefully. "I have no idea where she heard them, but she was close..." Her voice tightened. "She was close before they killed her."

"Mara died of black lung like half the dregs," Aeon said.

"Mara died of black lung, carried into her room in the folds of a dress, a gift from Makers Aspen and Larch."

"I didn't...Mara never...how do you...?" The words stuttered their way helplessly out of her mouth.

Tahl's face turned painfully kind. "Mara didn't want you to know. She was looking into crimes committed by Makers and you were made by one."

Aeon felt a wave of horror wash over her. "She suspected me?"

"No," Tahl said softly. "She didn't want to hurt you."

"How did you find out that they killed her?"

Tahl held Aeon's gaze. "I brought Sena into the palace, even though mother banned greenwives six years ago after that group of them tried to kill her. I was marched out and over the bridge as soon as the guards caught us, but not before Sena discovered what happened."

Aeon glanced across at the greenwife, who nodded gently and tried not to feel resentful that he had never told her. She couldn't expect someone who wasn't simulacra to understand the bond between an original and their fetch.

Had Mara even understood it? She had lied, hidden things, kept secrets from Aeon, from the person who shared her face, her life. All that kindness and laughter, had it all been a lie? But then that wasn't what Tahl had said.

She didn't want to hurt you.

They had killed Mara. Smeared black lung across the cloth of a dress. Black lung that clung to Mara's soft fingers as she moved, as she lifted her skirts, or brushed dirt from her bodice. Black lung that found its way inside her body, slipping in through her mouth, breathed in through her nose, burrowing its way inside her. Until the breath inside her spasmed, gasping out moment after stuttering moment, until she was suffocating in the thick black tar that had built up in her lungs. Until she was coughing, unable to stop coughing, drowning.

Aeon tried to ease her breathing, to still the panic and fury that threatened to burst out of her. They had killed her... Solel had killed Mara and then he had taken Aeon, used her in his vile experiments and almost killed her too. Aeon stared down at her bare arms. He had changed her forever. She had been proud her brands, of the pain she had endured when they were etched into her skin with ink and fire. They had been a mark of honour and of service. She had believed she would live and die with her original and he had taken even that from her.

Did he now dare to target the Empress herself? Did Solel really plan to kill the Empress Hira a'Tam and replace her with a copy?

Something shifted inside Aeon's chest. Era.

If Tahl's suspicions were right and Solel was targeting the Empress, then Aeon's caul-sister was in danger. She would die before she let them touch her original.

"Come on," Tahl said, rising briskly and startling Aeon out of her thoughts. "Banishment from the palace be hanged. I'm going to demand to see my mother and I'm going to tell her everything."

"You'll need proof," Sixfingers said. "Proof that they can do what you say they can."

Tahl grinned. "That's why I'm taking Aeon."

#

They walked briskly out into the wide, clean streets of the Tens District and the morning sunlight, heading for the market and the Imperial Bridge. Tahl moved swiftly through the bustling crowd, not looking behind her to see if Aeon followed.

The market was busy, hot and noisy. The air rich with the smells of the stalls and shop fronts. Hawkers and food sellers wandered the squares bellowing lurid descriptions of their wares, hampered by street entertainers, shop runners and crowds. The princess moved through the place like she owned it, which Aeon supposed in a way she did. Trailing behind, Aeon's gaze was caught by a flutter of paper on a notice wall beside a stall selling knitted slippers. The print smudged face that adorned it was sickeningly familiar.

Aeon darted forward, grabbing Tahl by the arm and pulling the hood of her coat over the head so that it shadowed her face.

Tahl shoved her away. "What in the Dark Mother's Domain?"

Aeon held up the paper, crumbled and torn from where she had tugged it down.

The princess's eyes went wide. "An arrest warrant!"

Aeon frowned down at the words. "It says you went mad and destroyed a Maker's workshop. That you've been driven insane by your sister's death and need to be placed under the urgent care of a doctor for the safety of yourself and others."

Tahl swore. "That…"

"This is Solel isn't it?" Bitterness filled Aeon's mouth. "We can't just walk into the palace now; the bridge guard will arrest you on sight. This is a Maker's warrant; they won't even take you to the Empress."

"I'm going to have him killed, slowly and painfully, while I watch." Tahl fumed, frustration warring with fear.

"There has to be another way."

Tahl grimaced. "There's always another way. Maybe if we —"

The marketplace erupted with sound. The shriek and squeal of grinding gears and tortured metal echoed from stone wall to stone wall, so loud and violent it hurt. Half the market crouched to the ground, hands over their ears. Beside

Aeon a child burst into tears.

Tahl turned and ran, mounting a flight of steps that lead up a brick and earth escarpment, an ancient defensive wall of the city now abandoned. From the higher vantage point she looked out over the city, shading her eyes against the glare of the sun. Aeon moved swiftly after her.

From the top of the wall they could see a fair number of the city bridges, including the one that led to the Imperial palace. Slowly, painfully, wailing and screaming, each one was rising, jerking back leaf by leaf, folding up over their windlasses house and creaking to an ominous halt.

"It's like curfew has come early," Aeon said softly.

Tahl swore so hard she nearly choked.

Not all the bridges were affected at once, and, as they and half the population of the city made a chaotic dash back to their own districts, Aeon managed to collar a bridge guard. He told her that there was some fault with the bridges and that the Makers had ordered them to be raised early so it could be investigated. Then, like the rest of the crowd, he ran.

Tahl and Aeon made it across to the Tens, just. The bridge rising howling and complaining behind them. When they reached Tahl's house, they found everyone, simulacra, greenwife and servants, gathered outside, their face's stark with shock.

Tahl stormed into the library and began to kick her own furniture.

Sena, standing in the doorway, folded his arms and stared meaningfully until she stopped. "We have to get into the palace," she said through clenched teeth. "This isn't a coincidence."

"We can't take a boat," Sixfingers said. "Even if the bridge guard don't catch us, the palace is built on top of razor walls, they'd cut us to shreds before we could get halfway up them."

Tahl kicked something else.

"I might have an idea about that," Naevus said.

"Really?" The princess turned round, she sounded incredulous.

"I'll have to make some inquiries."

"Do it," Tahl said tersely

Naevus went out and didn't come back until the late afternoon. They walked in looking tired and aggrieved and demanded a cup of khvā before they'd talk.

Tahl, who'd been pacing for hours, gestured sharply and servants brought in refreshment in delicate bone china cups. They gathered in what had become their usual seats in the library.

"The Imperial palace hasn't been infiltrated or attacked in over a hundred years, right?" Naevus began, cup in hand.

Tahl nodded tensely.

"And we know we can't go in over the water."

Sixfingers growled something.

Naevus's narrow face broke into a beatific smile. "So, let's try something the palace would never see coming in a thousand years. Something no one has dared try since the Bloody Armada was burnt to ashes."

"And what's that," Sixfingers grunted.

Naevus looked even more smug, if that were possible. "A cloudship."

#

Just after sunset, and obeying the nix's instructions, Aeon followed two rogue simulacra, a greenwife and the ninth princess of the Empire up the winding metal steps of a seaspire.

The spires were a natural phenomenon, standing scattered throughout the waters of the Empire. The great stacks of stone towered towards the sky; several stories above the tallest houses, they were the perfect place to build landing docks for cloudships. Each stack was complete with a set of winding metal steps accompanied by handrails bolted tightly into the stone and at their tips, the long, low metal platforms against which the cloud ships moored. Opposite each mooring station stood the great arms and windlasses to winch a ship's cargo down onto the waiting carts or boats that would carry it on into Tam City.

There were spires near each of the main city districts, connected to land by the broad fans of the Maker's bridges and patrolled by their own night watch. All except this one. Aeon peered up through a darkening sky, rent with gathering clouds, towards the distant height of the spire. Ragged metal and loops of chain showed in a shaft of the brother's white light. There was no bridge here, only cold, dark water and the small rowboat that bobbed them silently ever closer, Naevus and Sixfingers at the oars.

Aeon wondered what kind of illegal operation ran from the abandoned spire. Set close to the edge of the dregs, its platforms and haulage system had been damaged in a storm five years back, according to Naevus. The struggling traders who had been using it, moved on, leaving the spire to the elements, salt and wind and water.

They reached the dirty, half sunken quay, Sena stepping neatly out to throw a rope around a splintered piling. The wind had risen with the setting of the sun, gusting painfully over the open water and Aeon shivered despite the thickness of her cloak.

"Come on," Naevus muttered, craning their head back. "We've still got to get all the way up there."

The staircase was rusted, its handrail warped with steps missing in some places. The open sea was not kind to the things that people left to its mercy. Aeon gripped the rail, Sixfingers and Naevus front, Tahl and Sena behind, and began to climb.

"Don't worry." Sixfingers grinned down behind her, her face shadowed, and skull-like in the darkness. "If anyone's going to fall here, it'll be me."

The steps creaked ominously as she began to inch her way up, but they held. Aeon followed, looking for lights at the top of the spire but there was nothing but darkness and the scudding of clouds.

It felt like it took hours, before they reached the remains of the platform, legs shaking, and heads dizzy with the effects of the climb. Tahl and Sena were both gasping for breath and Aeon could feel the tug of effort on her own lungs. She let her ribs widen about her chest, increasing her lung capacity and took several deep, cleansing breaths. Beside her Sixfingers grinned.

Aeon turned to look at the cloudship.

It was unnaturally small, a wedge of dull grey envelope rising above a long, enclosed hull. Its engine looked like it was held together with ropes and a prayer. The name *Windsister's*

Secret was neatly painted on the bow.

A slight, lean figure leapt lightly down from the door of the cabin and made its way towards them. "Almost thought you weren't going to make it." A pale gaze swept across the huddled group. "This all of you?"

She had the warm brown skin, milk-pale hair and grey eyes of an uplander and looked about twelve. A moment later, a second figure climbed from the ship, just as slim and grey eyed. Twins. They both bore verdigris in curls of green-gold on their left hands, first finger for Lani, third finger for Lina. Aeon wondered where they had got the ink; she doubted they were imperial citizens.

Naevus introduced them with enthusiasm. "Lina, here, is a windsister- they know how to manage a sky craft. And Lani is a first-rate tiller hand."

Sena scowled. "Really?"

"We usually run cargo on the backwinds in and out of the further isles. Compared to that, this will be a doddle." It was Lani who spoke; like most windsisters, Lina was a little wind-tipped, and consequently hard to pin down. Windsisters were rare among the people of the Empire but common in the Vahiyaan uplands. Aeon wondered what had brought the twins all the way across the Bitter Sea to the Empire, where they would never be as respected as greenwives or bonedaughters. Demand for their skills with wind and wave had decreased dramatically after the Maker's bridges transformed the Empire into a landmass rather than a scattering of isles.

"Cargoes on the backwind, eh?" Sixfingers grinned. "Naev, you never told me you knew any smugglers?"

Lani grinned back. "Naev knows everyone."

"That doesn't explain why you're willing to do this," Tahl said frowning.

Lani met Tahl's narrowed gaze. "We owe Naev a life debt, and we uplanders pay our debts, Princess."

"You know who I am?"

"You think we'd fly this close to the palace's cloud-killers for just anyone?" Lani sad with no little contempt. The palace's battlements bristled with more cloud killing canon than there were spines on a poison eater. "Naevus says you ain't planning an assassination or the like, and all we have to do is drop you off."

The cloudship rocked slightly against its moorings in a breath of wind that was far gentler than the gust that had followed them on the short journey over. The ship's envelope was stretched tight, fashioned of some metal that was as delicate and flexible as fabric. Aeon would have thought it the work of a Maker if she hadn't known that all cloudships were made hundreds of miles away in Vahiyaa where there were no Makers.

"Come on," Lani beckoned as she made for the mooring ropes, uncoiling all but the one at the ship's middle. "Cover's almost ready."

Even as she spoke, clouds rushed up to cover the brother's pale form and the arch of the Dark Mother's Gate. Darkness slid over them.

A short ladder fashioned of metal rungs and rope shafts led up to a door oddly carved into the hull. The originals climbed up first, followed by the simulacra. Lani came last, leaning back from the open door to release the catch that held the final mooring rope. It fell away, as the cloudship lurched up from the dock and the soft hum of a firestone engine sounded from the back of the cabin.

"We usually have land crew to help with take-off and landing," Lani explained. "But we figured you wanted it discreet."

Naevus grinned. "Thanks, Lan."

The smuggler shrugged. "Make yourself comfortable, sit anywhere."

The cloudship was obviously not designed to carry passengers and the space inside the hull was awash with piles of rope, odd assortments of metal, several tattered canvases, and a variety of wooden boxes. No one asked any questions but found seating in silence. Looking from face to face Aeon wondered if the enormity of their plan had begun to hit the others. Sixfingers' hand kept sliding to the short blade she wore at her belt and Naevus alternated between biting their nails and running rough hands through their hair. Sena frowned uneasily out of the window and Tahl seemed to be looking anywhere but at anyone.

They're afraid. And they should be.

They were about to break into the Imperial Palace. If they were caught, they would die. Probably ignominiously.

But did they have a choice?

There was a traitor who wanted to replace the Empress with a puppet. He threatened Sena and Tahl's mother, Aeon's sister. He'd killed Roe and Fallow and the rest of Naevus' and Sixfingers' friends. Their family.

We all have reasons to be here.

She'd waited out a long night, crouched by Mara's bedside, listening to her breathing as it rasped, faded, faltered. She had felt the hand in hers grow cold, then colder, while all she could do was stand by and watch. All she could do was cling on for that one drawn out, last moment. She hadn't wanted to let go, but in the end, she had no choice. They had given her no choice, just as they had stolen away Sixfingers' lover and Naevus's friends.

Just as they threatened an Empire now.

"Almost there," Lani murmured softly. She was standing by the cabin entrance, apparently uncaring of the open doorway, the rush of wind and gust of air as the cloudship turned lazily over the spires and peaks of the city. The streets were bare, but lights twinkled in windows, blazing in the Scarlet District, where neither the gamblers at their tables of chance, nor the working Scarlets who entertained them, slept.

They passed over the open channels that separated the Districts, night waters drawing out a dark line between the pitched line of roofs and the gleam of lamplight. The bridges themselves stood in neatly folded lines above the chambers where their windlasses sat. The city was broken down into its independent working parts like disassembled clockwork scattered across a workbench, each island a solitary glimmer in the dark. Aeon shivered; it was not a comforting view.

As they neared the palace the fog came, dense and white, falling from above to blanket the world. The cloudship rose higher, moving out of range of the cloud killers, though Aeon doubted anyone could see them.

Sixfingers poked her head out of a nearby porthole and drew it back in sharply.

"The envelope's the colour of clouds," she announced. She sounded slightly dazed. Palace guards patrolled battlements and pathways as the *Windsister's Secret* passed silently overhead. But they didn't look up. Even if they had, they would have seen nothing but passing cloud and lowering fog.

They left the outer reaches of the palace, crossed over the Empress's Domain and reached the back of the palace; the small, mean dwellings where servants were sent when they were no longer needed.

Lani was dropping coils of black rope from the doorway as Lina held the cloudship steady. They slid down through the air and hit the nearest wall with soft slaps.

Lani glanced across at Naevus. "Sure, you don't need us to wait?"

Naevus shook their head. "Get out of here. If we leave the palace tonight it won't be by cloudship."

Lani narrowed her eyes but gave the nix a tight smile.

Aeon followed her friends to the door, watching as, one by one, they dropped away into the dark. She watched until it was her turn and then she was grasping hard to the slick rope. She was climbing downwards, hand over hand, the rope swaying unnervingly beneath her. The night opened up to swallow her whole.

#

For a moment Aeon clung to the wall, grateful for the steadiness beneath her feet. The night was a shadow about her, close and soft as silk. A hand on her shoulder and she jumped. It was Sixfingers, moving surprisingly quietly for someone so large. Her face was taut with warning, bright eyes hard. Naevus appeared a little further along, huddled between

Sena and Tahl. For a moment Aeon just looked at them, these people. She had known none of them a month ago and there was a good chance she was going to die with them tonight. No one survived breaking into the Imperial Palace, surely.

Tahl gestured, long fingers a blur in the darkness. This way.

Aeon prayed to all the Mothers that the princess was right, that this close to the Empress's personal domain, those that stood in their way would take them to the Empress herself instead of throwing them into the unknown depths of the Imperial dungeons.

Aeon stepped up, moving to walk shoulder to shoulder with Sixfingers. The fist was frowning, her bright eyes sweeping the shadows as they moved, but there was an ease in her too. As if she knew this and it was not something she was afraid of. Aeon doubted she gave off that kind of confidence. They reached Naevus, who glanced up with a silent grin. Then everyone was hurrying through the empty palace in the ninth princess's wake.

Of course, they were going to get caught. This was the inner sanctum of the most powerful woman in the Bitter Sea. Her servants were sharp and attentive, her guards alert at every corner, patrolling in patterns with every phase of the clock.

They headed for the Empress's private audience hall.

It felt like hours of peering round corners and slinking through doorways before they reached the ornate corridor and the tall double doors whose etched metal was inlaid with mother-of-pearl that gleamed like oil on water and coral so delicate that light glowed through it.

Tahl had calculated the change of the guards down to the second and Sena's fingertips glowed faintly emerald as he worked to shield them from the casual glances of passing servants.

"I can't make you invisible," he had said, when they sat in Tahl's house discussing the plan. "But as long as no one looks too closely we will seem like shadows crossing the floor."

Like shadows. No wonder the Makers had created simulacra. Aeon suppressed a shiver.

Still, no one stopped them as they approached the doors and a pair of cold-eyed guards. Tahl shot Sena a glance and the glow across his fingers died away.

"What are we doing now?" Sixfingers muttered.

"It's all right, they've known me since I was born," Tahl hissed back.

She strode forward.

"Malorc, Gitya." She nodded coolly. The guards jumped, eyes widening as she appeared of nowhere. "I need to speak to my mother."

The audience chamber was just as it had been on the morning the Empress had thanked Aeon for her service and sent her away to her end. Only, instead of golden sunlight it was flooded with the yellow glow of stone lamps. And the Empress, in a sleeping robe and wrapped in a silk shawl, looked far from magnanimous. Her large, dark eyes, so like Mara's, were cold as she stared down at them from the golden lines of her throne. Malorc and Gitya had retreated to the door, where they stood like statues. Spears held ready in brown, calloused hands. Aeon tried to ignore them, but the back of her neck itched with apprehension.

"Daughter," The Empress said, her tone expressionless.

"Mother." Tahl bowed neatly, a timely display of deference.

"I believe you were informed that you are no longer welcome in the palace."

"And I would not dare to disobey you, Mother, if it were not vitally important that I speak with you."

The Empress's expression did not change. "How did you get in?"

Tahl flushed. "I had help."

"They are traitors." The Empress's gaze swept the room. Aeon could feel the deathly chill of her gaze. "As are all you who stand here."

"Mother!"

"No, Tahl. You have defied me at every turn, and I, like a fond fool, let you. But you have gone against my word for the last time and I –,"

"You don't understand." The words fell hollow into the stillness, stopping the Empress cold. Aeon wasn't even quite sure they had fallen from her mouth.

The Empress turned on her. "You stand there with my dead daughter's face and dare to speak. How is it you stand here at all? You were to be ended."

Aeon glanced down at her bare arms. "Solel a'Vari found a better use for me."

"Really? And what use would that be? Solel is an Apprentice not a Maker."

"He was an Apprentice," Sena muttered.

The words drew the Empress attention and Aeon watched the shock that rippled through her dark gaze. There was no mistaking the greenwife for anything but Tahl's brother. They were of a height, with the same wide spaced eyes, even if his were a gleaming green and hers were a warm, wary brown.

Same nose, same mouth, even their chins matched.

The Empress stared down at her abandoned son and said nothing.

Tahl tried again. "Mother, you must listen. I have brought —"

The shadows by the double doors moved. It was unnervingly swift, a pool of ink moving from a spill across the floor to upright figures in a moment. Six figures, a tall, slender man in a bronze Maker's mask, an older man who seemed faintly familiar, with the verdant eyes of a greenwife, and four broad shouldered shapes in long cloaks and lowered hoods The fourth figure moved like a simulacra, but Aeon knew that he wasn't. None of them were.

"Master Maker! Explain yourself!" The Empress's voice snapped out through the sudden stillness of the room even as Tahl stepped between the throne and the new arrivals. Sixfingers and Naevus moved up to flank her and Sena's fingertips shimmered with wildfire.

The Maker bowed smooth and low, blue eyes gleaming warmly behind the curled edges of the bronze mask. Aeon swallowed the sudden rise of fear, seeing him standing here, in the audience chamber of the Empress, taking on that name as if he owned it. If that was true how could a few rogue simulacra, an outcast and a rebellious princess stand against him?

"Majesty," Solel said softly. "I have a matter of great urgency to put before you. I apologise for the late hour. But I see you have guests."

"They were just leaving," the Empress said.

"I am not," Tahl said stoutly. "Mother, you cannot trust him."

"The Maker who has served me faithfully for my entire reign? The Maker who served my mother and her mother before her? Do you really think being my ninth daughter makes you more worthy than he?"

Tahl turned to her mother, her face hard with desperation. "But I am your daughter, Mother. I only want to protect you."

The Empress sighed, her face softening for a moment. "Child, I do not need your protection. I am Empress. I have guards at my door. I have half a hundred swordbreakers at my call." She gestured with a flick of long, pale fingers and Era stepped out from behind the throne. Aeon felt a sudden thrill of relief as if she had been holding her breath without realising it. "I have my fetch," she glanced across at her son. "Should a greenwife turn their cursed-eye upon me."

From her place beside the throne Era glanced around the room, bowing briefly. Her gaze flickered when it passed over Aeon. Her expression did not change, although a shiver of distress showed in her dark eyes.

She has been mourning me all this time. She thought me ended.

Aeon resisted the urge to cross the room and offered a smile instead. When this was over, they would have a long, comfortable talk. She would tell Era everything.

"I will ask you one more time, Tahl," the Empress said. Her tone was calm, but her face was hard. "Will you leave?"

Tahl glanced across at Aeon and appeared to read something in her face. The princess' gaze slid past Sixfingers and Naevus to look at her brother, who nodded solemnly.

"No," she said. "We will not."

"That," Solel said, "is unfortunate."

The Empress turned her head.

Solel pulled the mask from his face.

The gear-corps moved without apparent instruction. For dead flesh made animate they moved uncannily fast. Two breaths, maybe three and the guards at the door were down, their blood pooling out across the tiled floor. Tahl cried out, a wordless sound. The gear-corps turned towards her as Solel's greenwife flung back his cloak. Aeon placed him then; he was Bleak, Master Larch's doorkeep. All the time she had known him, he had hidden his eyes. Sena had said that Makers worked with greenwives. This one, she was quickly realising, belonged to Solel.

Green wildfire flared as Bleak raised his hands. Sena left his sister's side, facing his fellow curse-worker, his own fire flaring.

The gear-corps had reached Sixfingers and Naevus.

And Aeon had her own problems.

The fourth figure was heading straight for her, flinging back his cloak to reveal a deadly litheness, a swordbreaker's grace and a speed greater than her own. Aeon had never used a sword. She was a fetch; she and her original relied on the escapement beneath her skin, the grinding wind of tooth and gear.

Solel's thrall was an original, taken and changed by Maker's skill into something akin to a gear-corpse but faster and more deadly.

The thrall came at her, arms raised. He held a weapon in each hand, a longer knife flanked by a pair of shorter tines. No, not held, the weapons grew from the back of his hands like straight, steel roots, each blade was razor sharp and glinted in the lamplight.

It must hurt; blood ran down his fingers, but he barely seemed to notice.

A blade sliced the air in front of Aeon's face, and she leapt back, feet skidding on the smooth floor. A tined blade slid through the air a breath from her face and she was scrambling frantically backwards, the sound of her own heart ringing in her ears.

She heard Naevus cry out but didn't dare turn and look, darting behind a side table to avoid another slice. Her attacker made no sound, dark eyes burning into her face as he moved.

The Empress was shouting. Aeon couldn't understand the words, but she seemed furious rather than frightened. Tahl's voice answered. Sixfingers swore and the screech of steel on bronze echoed through the room. Aeon flung a vase at her attacker and, when he ducked, glanced back to see Sixfingers pulling her sword from the cog-rack of a gear-corpse. Black fluid leaked from its skull. Naevus was crumpled at her feet and the other gear-corpse was facing Tahl. The princess held a determined look and a poker in one hand.

Aeon heard the hiss of a blade and ducked again, turning to slam her whole body into her opponent. Surprised, he staggered back, and she kicked at his knee. He slid sideways and her foot found thin air. She lurched forward, almost fell, pulling herself upright just as his blade slipped into her side.

Bright pain burst behind her eyes.

The thrall let her go and she fell, hitting the floor hard, sparks juddering up her spine. White light throbbed from her hip to her ribs and her breath was shallow, gasping as she dragged in air.

Her opponent stepped over her, blades held low, one slick

with her blood.

He walked towards the Empress.

Aeon blinked. She was suddenly so tired, the air cool against her skin. Sixfingers shouted somewhere in the distance and further away the sound of banging rang out, servants or guards trying to open the doors on which Solel had planted his one remaining gear-corpse. The bulk of the dead man held the doors easily. There would be no help from the Empress' forces.

Aeon turned her head and watched Tahl and Sixfingers as they stood back to back. Sixfingers was fighting the gear-corpse that had downed Naevus and Tahl was facing Aeon's wordless opponent.

Solel stood back from the fighting, watching as his forces cut their way to the Empress. From the floor, one hand clutched hard to her side, Aeon saw Sena sink to his knees, Bleak cackling as wildfire sizzled above his head.

Solel stepped away from the wall.

He moved like liquid through the room and Era moved to meet him. Aeon struggled to rise, to call out a warning. He was dangerous, more dangerous to Era who knew him only as their Maker's Apprentice, who'd known him when he was a shy youth just finding his way.

He's not who you think he is.

Aeon opened her mouth to shout but no words came out. It hurt to breathe.

In the middle of the room, Solel gazed down at Era. "It's time," he said.

Chapter Seven

Era smiled, her face, the Empress's face, cool as early snow. "Are you sure?"

Solel's face was hidden beneath his mask but he reached into a pocket, pulling out a slim, wooden box. "Yes."

As one Simulacra and Maker turned to look up at the Empress on the throne.

"Aeon."

Warm, careful hands were on her shoulders, holding a little too tight. She pulled her head round and found a pair of wide, green eyes. For a moment she panicked, jerking back, biting back a gasp of terror. Then she saw soft, brown skin, curling hair and Tahl's nose and chin.

"S…S…"

"No, don't try to speak, just give me a moment." The greenwife's eyes narrowed, his hands flaring with sudden heat. Flames tricked over Aeon's skin, heating the cold place where the thrall had slipped in his blade.

For an instant the flames were inside her, burning, hungry. Then she felt the whirr and click of jolted clockwork, a shiver of deeply buried mechanisms. And then she was sitting up, coughing and swearing, her pain gone.

Sena grinned. "It's so much easier to fix..." He trailed off.

Simulacra. The word seemed to hover for a moment, unsaid.

Aeon grabbed his hands. "Help Naevus," she said.

The greenwife went and Aeon clambered to her feet. Tahl and Sixfingers were still fighting and even if Sixfingers could kill a second gear-corpse, Aeon doubted even princess and fist together could hold against Solel's new invention.

Moments later Tahl staggered back, swearing, her shirt slick with blood.

The princess might be holding out, but the thrall moved almost too fast to see and never seemed to tire. And if Tahl fell there would be nothing to protect Sixfingers' back.

Aeon glanced round the rest of the room. One gear-corpse at the door, solid as a boulder but under orders to do nothing but stand there. Bleak lay on the floor, not two feet from her. Aeon did not know what Sena had done but Solel's greenwife lay with the boneless stillness of the dead. His face was blackened and charred, his green eyes staring at nothing.

Solel had brought serum and needles with him. Aeon was sure that was what sat in the box he had brandished at Era... Era! Aeon shoved that thought away. There was no time for it now. No time to wonder if she had ever known her sister at all.

Aeon shook her head and crossed the room, crouching down to rifle through the pockets of Solel's greenwife. There it was; a slim wooden box. A back up?

Bleak had to be the curse-worker who attacked Tahl in the Maker's house.

Aeon opened the box; glass and bronze gleamed back at

her. Tiny, glass vials glittered in the lamplight. One black, the purge. One greenish-gold. No split shot. Aeon swore but there was no time for anything else. She picked up the first syringe with shaking fingers.

The purge burned through her, sending her heaving into a corner to empty her stomach of everything that was in it. The acrid smell stung her eyes and left her panting, but she turned away. She pulled out a second syringe and a second vial.

Tahl screamed, half fury, half pain and Aeon turned to see Sixfingers and the princess side by side, backing slowly away from the thrall. He was slowed in his own advance by the jerky, uneven movements of the gear-corpse that Sixfingers had somehow impaled on the shattered leg of an upturned table.

Aeon inched closer. She had to move before the thrall realised that she was there. She would only have seconds and there would only be one attempt.

She forced her hands to stop trembling.

The thrall lifted his blades. Sixfingers stepped away from the princess, standing ready, her own blade raised. Tahl was bleeding from several gashes in her arms and legs. Her poker wavered desperately, and she was sobbing with every breath.

The thrall looked at her and smiled.

Aeon crept along the wall; reached the table, ducked under the flailing gear-corpse and leapt, arms raised. One arm wrapped round the thrall's neck, the other hand dug the syringe in between his shoulder blades. Aeon drew the plunger back with her teeth.

The thrall staggered under her and Aeon kicked off, using the momentum to push them apart and slam the thrall into the ground.

"Get to the Empress," she gasped, jamming the syringe into her own arm and pressing the plunger down.

She dropped as the flames of change rolled over her, heat building inside as the world outside went dark.

\#

"Isn't this pretty? Such a kind gift." Mara whirled and the skirts of the dress whirled with her. "Won't it be perfect for mother's banquet?"

Aeon thought it was too sombre in colour, the fabric heavy against the princess's pale skin. But she said nothing.

Mara looked up. "There's something I need to tell you, later. After the banquet. Will you stay up until I get back?"

"Yes, Highness."

Mara laughed, warm and deep. "Mara, remember. It's always Mara. I'll see you tonight."

She blew Aeon a kiss and swirled away in her brand-new gown.

\#

Aeon did not wake, instead the darkness receded like a tide, leaving light and awareness behind. Without moving Aeon reached out to interrogate the shapes and lines of the new body. Broad shoulders, a tapered waist. There were muscles under the flesh of this body, a strength and speed like nothing Aeon had ever felt. Aeon lifted a hand and looked at the lines of green ink that twined delicately down the soft, brown skin of his middle finger.

He pulled himself carefully up into a sitting position,

working to move in this unfamiliar shape. The feeling would pass, but at this moment Aeon and the body were not quite one.

The air tasted of blood and there was something moving beneath the broad backs of his new hands. Aeon frowned, tilted his hands and watched as the blades slid out. The buzz of pain was sharp but momentary. The two slim blades, flanked by a pair of short, sharp tines, were obviously ossium. Aeon felt along his left arm for the half-submerged form of his escapement – it was gone. So was the escapement on his right, repurposed by the change into the foot-long blades.

Aeon climbed awkwardly to his feet, remembering in a rush where he was and what was happening. A moment later the tip of a blade dug into the tiles at his feet, spraying shards across his legs. Aeon ignored the smarting pain and looked up to meet a pair of blank, black eyes. His eyes now. Aeon stiffened, holding the empty gaze without flinching and lifted his blades.

He slid forward, slicing the air, twisting his shoulder to throw his whole weight behind it. The thrall spun away but not fast enough. Aeon's blade found bare flesh, and the thrall hissed as he stumbled backwards, wrenching his blade from the ground.

Aeon followed.

The thrall was used to his body, he knew its strengths and weaknesses, he had worked for that muscle and speed. Aeon had only one advantage. It wasn't his body; it wasn't his face. It was a weapon he had taken up for the fight and whether it bled or broke or died meant nothing to him. It couldn't matter. All that mattered was stopping the thrall.

Wordless noises spilled from Aeon's mouth as he surged across the room, sword soundless as it cut the air. The thrall snarled, lifting his blades as Aeon whirled towards him. Steel met steel in a clash of metal and a cascade of sparks.

The thrall spun upwards and Aeon followed him, catching the downward stroke of a killing blow on the tines of his left hand. The force rippled through his body and his arm went numb, but his grip did not falter. The thrall thrust low with his right blade, but Aeon was already moving, his body knew how to respond, copying in perfect eerie symmetry the skills of its original.

That was why Solel's plan would work. Simulacra were perfect copies; form; voice; movement. Without the snaking red, green and gold of their brands, without their Maker's seal, they could be their original.

Aeon met his opponent's stroke and turned it, kicking out with a booted foot that sent the thrall staggering backwards again.

Just as Aeon was the thrall's match.

Behind the thrall, the great arc of the throne towered and, in its shadow, Tahl and Sixfingers stood, blade and poker in hand. Before them, on the steps of the throne, Solel stood between two Empresses, a hand on each. They were both tall, dark haired, dark eyed and cold featured. Their arms were bare to the shoulder and pale as milk. Unmarked. Aeon could see the indecision on Tahl's face and the fury on Sixfingers.

Then the thrall darted in and all Aeon could think of was block and parry, attack and move. Together they danced, round and round the hall, blade to blade, bodies shifting with breathless grace.

In that moment all Aeon knew was the dance, his body reacting, remembering the skills it had learnt. Years of dedication and training, hour after hour of form and pattern. Days without food, nights without sleep.

Who was this thrall?

Aeon pressed on, not daring to stop, not daring to hesitate. The blades wove against each other, sending the glow of lamplight out in patterns across the ceiling. The air was full of the clash of steel and the stink of blood.

The moment came without warning. The thrall must have been tiring for he slipped, and Aeon pressed forward, taking the advantage. His blade moved as if with its own will, slicing through leather and cloth, through flesh and bone, to send the thrall crashing to the ground. Aeon crouched, swung again, blow weighted with fury and grief. It sheared through the delicate edge of the thrall's sword, snapping it just below the line of his fingers. Blood and ossium mingling together on the red-slicked floor.

The thrall was panting and sweat-soaked, his lips twisted in a snarl of defeat. One leg twisted at an unnatural angle.

He did not rise.

Aeon looked down into his empty eyes for one moment, then stepped past, making for the throne on aching legs. Behind him the sound of metal against wood rang out. The Empress's men had found a battering ram. At the door, the lone gear-corpse grunted and spread its legs wider, straining to hold back the tide.

Sena joined Aeon as he reached the shadow of the throne. "Naevus?"

The greenwife smiled, though he was clearly exhausted, his

face pale, dark shadows like bruises beneath the glow of his eyes. "Comfortable, they should recover."

The thought: *if we survive* remained unspoken.

Aeon nodded. He flexed his fingers, letting the crisp, perfectly balanced mechanism grafted onto the bones of his hand draw the blades back inside his flesh. When they were gone, he could not feel them at all. Unlike the escapement that had been ever present beneath the skin and flesh, they were simply – gone.

He curled his fists and went to face his Maker.

#

"The council of the Ten will never let a simulacra rule," Tahl was protesting as Aeon and Sena approached.

Solel shrugged. "Tell me, which is the Empress and which the copy? Who will they believe, Princess, a ninth daughter who has never done as she was told or a Master Maker renowned and respected for centuries?"

Aeon had wondered why the Empress had neither spoken nor moved, while her daughter and rogue simulacra fought for her throne and her life. But as he drew closer, the taste of metal flooded his mouth and the air crackled against his ears. The Maker's hand was not simply resting on the shoulders of the two Empresses. He was holding them in place, they were caught in a spell just as Fallow's body had been, frozen, unmoving.

The Empress could not speak for herself; she could not speak at all.

"Let them go." Sixfingers' blade was angled towards the

Maker and was steady in her hand even though Aeon knew, her stomach must be crawling with dread. Rogue simulacra hid from their Makers or they ran from them, they did not turn and fight. Solel had already walked into Sixfingers' home and slaughtered her friends. He had nearly killed her. Did she even know that Sena had helped Naevus? Had she looked behind her and seen that her friend was safe? Was she expecting to die here, at the hands of this man?

Aeon moved to stand at the fist's left side. Sixfingers glanced sideways, eyes widening slightly before she caught Aeon's gaze and grinned.

The Maker glanced from Sixfingers to Aeon and frowned.

"What are you waiting for?" he said. "Kill her."

Aeon held his gaze. "I don't think I'm who you think I am," he said.

For a moment the Maker blinked and then he swore, his hands tightening reflectively in the shoulders of both Empress and simulacra. Their bones creaked audibly under the pressure. Aeon flinched.

"You defeated my thrall with a trick. Do you think that will save your Empress or your sister?" He sneered.

But Aeon had watched Solel's body tense, his jaw tightening. He could all but smell the Maker's fear.

"It's no trick. I am the thrall, I'm just not under your command. Why is Era working with you?"

"She's tired of living in the shadow of her original. And it's fair; she's clever, quick, strong. Why shouldn't she make her own mark on the world?"

"By stealing an Empire?"

Solel shrugged. "If needs be."

Tahl's eyes narrowed. "Is it her Empire or yours, Maker?"

But then Tahl didn't know Era. Aeon had no trouble believing that his caul-sister would be the one doing the ruling.

"What do you get out of it, Maker?" Aeon did not bother to keep the contempt from his voice.

"I get a charter that allows me to build and sell gear-corps and thralls both in the Empire and abroad." He spoke as if the answer was obvious - which Aeon supposed it was.

"And you'll get all the dead bodies and puppets you need from the dregs I suppose."

Solel shrugged. "It's not as if anyone will miss them."

Aeon thought of the house on the edge of the broken pier, green fire liming its windows and roof as the pilings failed and it plunged into the ocean. That house had been a home, the people who lived there a family. Most of them were dead now. But there were other houses like that, other families scattered across the fragments of island that made up the dregs. Some of them would be rogue simulacra running from their Makers' rule and some of them would be the clockwork city's lost, abandoned with nowhere else to go. And in not one of their houses, not one of those families, would anyone disappear unmourned and unmissed. If Solel didn't understand that then he understood nothing, about either simulacra or originals.

Aeon glared at the mask that covered Solel's face. The Apprentice had claimed it for himself, taken it by force from the man who had offered a home to a shy and hesitant boy and taught him everything he knew. Maker Larch had not deserved that. He had done nothing to invite such a betrayal.

There is nothing he will not do to get what he wants.

Him and Era.

"You've lost the Empress. Accept it." Solel said softly. He flexed his fingers, releasing the spell. Both Empresses fell to their knees at the same time, their breath gasping out in the cool night air.

Because we breathe just like any original.

And there were some things even Solel's serum couldn't change.

"I don't think we have," Aeon said.

He moved in the way of all simulacra, smooth as silk between one blink and the next, there was no way Solel could avoid him. With one hand he grabbed the wrist of the nearest Empress, jerking her close, while with the other he drew the sharp edge of a tine down her bare arm, hard enough to part skin and reveal the flesh beneath. The Empress gasped, pulling at Aeon's grip, but he was stronger than any fetch. Era was still struggling when the golden glint of her escapement emerged between wet blood and red flesh for all to see.

One Solel's other side, the Empress began to crawl away, still gasping for breath. The Maker caught her with a fist in her hair, dragging her backwards. She hissed, fighting his grip until a blade was pressed across her bare throat.

Sixfingers swore.

Tahl gripped her poker so hard her knuckles turned white and Aeon did not dare let go of Era, not for an instant. She was pale and in obvious pain, but she battled him as fiercely as the Empress fought Solel.

"Let my mother go, Maker," Tahl hissed.

"If I let her go, I'm dead." The Maker's voice was matter of fact.

"You're dead either way." The Empress's voice was laden

with pain, tinged with panicked, but it did not waver – she meant what she said.

Solel glanced across at Era. Aeon could almost hear him thinking as his gaze drifted through the room. His greenwife was dead, his thrall a crumpled body on the floor. Two of his three gear-corps dead and the third struggling to keep the Empress's desperate guards from the room.

"There's no way out," Tahl said.

Solel moved quickly, so quickly that even Aeon did not see the moment when the blade bit down. He saw only the blood and the Empress falling. Tahl started forward with a cry, Sena a step behind her, his hands already glowing green with wildfire.

Sixfingers ran Solel through with a single thrust, her blade sliding into his chest and emerging from his back in a gout of blood.

The Maker fell, warm blue eyes wide and empty, staring sightlessly at the arc of the ceiling above them.

A second later the final gear-corpse fell too. Without the Maker he was nothing but a dead body and a lot of fancy gear-work.

The door was clear.

Aeon didn't wait for the palace guard to break in, he headed for the back of the room instead, to the door that waited behind the Empress's throne, dragging his sister behind him.

#

Beyond the throne everything was quiet, though the smell of blood had permeated even here. Aeon's grip on Era's arm tightened as he swung her round to face him in the dim lamplight. She did not look remorseful, but she did look afraid.

"She was your original!"

"I was less than a servant to her, a thing she owned like a table, or a useful kitchen implement."

"She is an Empress, Era. I doubt she's ever used a kitchen implement in her life."

A faint smile curved Era's lips. "I wanted to be real," she said, "I wanted to be…someone."

"You are someone. You are my sister; you are my friend; you were the fetch of the most powerful woman in the Bitter Sea."

Era shrugged, her bright gaze dropping away. "It wasn't enough."

"What about Mara? What about my original. Were you a part of her murder?"

Era looked away. "I liked her," she said softly. "I didn't wish her harm."

Which didn't mean anything, not really.

"You know what your original's going to do now, don't you?"

Era swallowed. "She will turn to me over to one of the other Makers and they will end me."

"Execution is the punishment for all traitors."

Aeon stared down into his sister's face. It was strange to be taller than her, they had been of a height for so long. But Aeon had chosen the purging shot, chosen to give Mara up, to save his friends and stop Solel. The thrall's face was all the face he had now – unless he found someone willing to give him their likeness and ask for nothing in return. That was not something that any original would do for a simulacra.

Still, he had no regrets.

After a long moment Era said, "You're going to let me go, aren't you?"

"Hira will hunt you down. You have her face; it won't be hard to find you."

Era slid her arm very gently from Aeon's grasp, he did not try and stop her.

She reached up, dropping a warm kiss on his cheek. "Thank you, brother," she said. And then so softly Aeon could barely hear the words. "I'm sorry."

A moment later, she was gone.

#

"My mother is always saying I need a simulacra," Tahl said with a wry smile as they followed a silent, neatly clad servant up the grand staircase to the second floor where the family chambers were situated.

"I doubt this was what the Empress had in mind," Sixfingers said dryly and the princess laughed.

Aeon wasn't sure how he felt about the bedchamber or the invitation to make his home under the protection of the ninth princess. Naevus had refused outright, vanishing back into the jumble of islands that made up the dregs. They had to inform the twins of the *Windsister's Secret* that they were still alive, and besides, originals and royalty made them nervous.

"If you ever need me, or just want to share a cup for old time's sake, leave word at the Moth," they said. The nix and the greenwife left together; there was talk about finding a new house.

Sixfingers was quieter than Aeon had ever known her. There was a taut line in her jaw and a hollowness lurked behind her eyes that never quite left. Aeon had been surprised when she didn't choose to leave with Naevus and Sena. But she seemed to find peace and comfort in the ordered luxury of the princess's domain.

And in the princess, herself. The few times Aeon had seen Sixfingers laugh over the last three weeks had been in Tahl's company. It was too early for anything more than common ground and the sharing of dry wit, but Tahl seemed to appreciate the fist in her turn. Her gaze grew warm every time she looked at the tall, broad shouldered warrior.

Aeon wasn't sure where he stood in the household or even if he would stay. Maybe he could find a home among the hard, sharp people of the dregs. Naevus had offered. The rogue simulacra in the house on Swallow Street had shielded Aeon from the world beyond their door. They had shared kindness, laughter and khvā without a thought or asking for anything in return. But they were gone now, all but two. There was nothing left of that safety.

When he'd returned to the audience hall, without Era, he found it thronged with guards, servants and pale looking courtiers who obviously did not know what to think or do. Aeon didn't need Tahl to tell him they were members of the council.

The bodies were laid out on the floor in a row. The gear-corps were already beginning to smell and Solel looked smaller somehow without his Maker's mask. Aeon had never seen him so still. Of the thrall whose face Aeon now shared there was no sign. No doubt Solel's puppetry had failed when he died, just as the life had vanished from the gear-corps. The Empress sent guards to search the palace and grounds, but he, just like Era, was gone.

The Empress commanded that likenesses of both the nameless thrall and her own rogue simulacra to be posted throughout the Empire. Aeon had even allowed an imperial artist to capture his likeness on paper for the print, after extracting a sealed letter from the Empress declaring his innocence. So far there had been no word.

The man had been an ensorcelled of course, he had not chosen to turn traitor. But Aeon couldn't quite forgive him for the slaughter on Swallow Street. He was sure that it was the thrall's blades that had punctured Roe and Glints' skulls, that had nearly killed Sixfingers.

He was still getting used to wearing the man's face. Every time he looked in a mirror, he expected to see Mara's eyes, her pale skin, her smile – instead a stranger stared back. Sixfingers suggested that Aeon hire himself out as Glint and Talon had done, until he found himself a face more to his liking. But Aeon had no wish to stand fetch for anyone else; he wasn't even sure he could do it anymore with his escapement gone to make blades. It was what he had been created for, but he couldn't bear to be as close to anyone as he had been to his princess.

The thrall was gone, Aeon could choose his own path. He could be…someone. Wasn't that what all simulacra wanted, deep down: to be real? He couldn't even begrudge Era that wish.

"So," Tahl threw her arms wide. "Enough of sleeping in guest quarters. Pick any room on this floor – it's yours. Mirna has set you up with a line of credit. I will pay you a salary of two crowns a year, including food and board."

Sixfingers frowned, peering into a richly appointed room with heavy brocade hangings on the wall and thick, brightly patterned Ilarian rugs on the floor.

"A wage?"

The princess shrugged. "You have to be able to live."

"I'm a rogue simulacra, and a fist from the dregs. I've never even seen a crown in my life, let alone two. But I won't take money for nothing."

Tahl smiled softly. "Fool, do you think my mother was wrong to want to give me protection? I'm a stubborn soul who spends far too much time among gamblers and whores, not to mention the nobles of the court. I need bodyguards."

Aeon raised an eyebrow; he had not known this face could do that. "Bodyguards?"

"It's rare to find a warrior who can't be disarmed." Tahl grinned mischievously. "What do you say?"

Aeon glanced across at Sixfingers. One side of her mouth was tipped up in a half smile.

"Well," Aeon said slowly. "If you're sure."

www.ingramcontent.com/pod-product-compliance
Lightning Source LLC
Chambersburg PA
CBHW030828200726
48285CB00007B/2397